THE LONELY ONE

Recent Titles by Claire Rayner from Severn House

CHILDREN'S WARD
COTTAGE HOSPITAL
THE DOCTORS OF DOWNLANDS
THE FINAL YEAR
THE LONELY ONE
NURSE IN THE SUN
THE PRIVATE WING

THE
LONELY ONE

Claire Rayner

This edition published in Great Britain 1995 by
SEVERN HOUSE PUBLISHERS LTD of
9–15 High Street, Sutton, Surrey SM1 1DF.
First published in Great Britain 1965 in paperback format
only under the pseudonym of Sheila Brandon. This edition
revised and entirely reset.

British Library Cataloguing in Publication Data
Rayner, Claire
    Lonely One. – New ed
    I. Title
    823.914 [F]

    ISBN 0-7278-4753-8

Typeset by Hewer Text Composition Services, Edinburgh.
Printed and bound in Great Britain by
Hartnolls Ltd, Bodmin, Cornwall.

Chapter 1

Bridget sat at the desk at the very end of the back row, staring round the big classroom with miserable eyes. The letter from Matron had told her to arrive at the Preliminary Training School at 2 p.m., and she had decided then that she would try to be the first to arrive. She had a confused notion that the other new girls would arrive accompanied by loving parents, and she wanted to make sure that this time at least she would not have to face the pitying eyes of people who realised she had no parents. All through her schooldays she had shrunk from that all too familiar look on the faces of other girls and their parents, and although she knew quite well that it was no fault in her to be without a mother and father of her own, she felt an obscure sense of shame about it. So she had decided to arrive early, letting later arrivals think her parents had already left.

But, as always seemed to happen to Bridget, her plans had been almost too well laid. She had arrived at just after one, and the little maid who answered the door to her had led her into the classroom and told her to wait there for Sister Tutor.

'You're too early,' the maid had said, somewhat crossly, humping Bridget's big suitcase into the classroom and dropping it with a clatter on to the polished floor. 'Sister's having her lunch, and I better not disturb her – she'll be flaming mad if I do – ' and Bridget, stumbling over her words, had begged the girl to please *not* disturb Sister Tutor, she was fine, really she was,

1

please do not bother about her – And the maid had looked at her with ill-disguised contempt in her eyes, or so Bridget had thought, and gone off with a shrug to finish the illicit cup of tea she had been drinking in the kitchen.

And now Bridget sat and looked about her, frightened as always by the newness of things, for Bridget was not a girl to find strange surroundings exciting. For her, newness was menacing, something to be faced with screwed-up courage, not pleasure. In one way, the room had a school-like familiarity – the rows of desks, the teachers' dais backed by a blackboard, the smell of chalk and ink, and faint overtones of human bodies that had spent long hours here.

But there were other things in the room that made it utterly strange. The three hospital beds against one wall; the cupboards, glass fronted, white enamelled and chromed, showing rows of instruments, bowls, piles of wound dressings; the charts on the walls depicting very unhuman-looking men and women, with their muscles and organs all too faithfully drawn in ugly blues and reds, and the articulated skeleton that dangled from the little hook in its skull from a big metal stand.

Bridget giggled aloud, a little hysterically, at him, and said softly, 'I wish I were you – ' but the skeleton just hung and grinned mockingly at her.

There was silence, not even a faint clatter of human movement coming from the rest of the building behind the closed door of the classroom. With an effort, Bridget got to her feet, and started to prowl about the room, looking at the strange things, running her fingers over the desks she passed, trying to gain a sense of security from touching these calm inanimate objects.

She stopped in front of one of the glass-fronted cabinets, peering at its contents with a sort of fascinated horror. There were gleaming scalpels, dangling rows of artery forceps, big metal loops that were retractors, though Bridget had not the faintest idea what they were for, let alone what they were called. Tentatively, she put her hand on the fastening of the glass door, and it swung open on well-oiled hinges. With one slightly shaking finger she touched one of the rows of artery forceps that hung from below one of the shelves, and as she did so, the big door of the classroom opened with a sharp click, and someone came in.

Bridget whirled to see who it was, and her convulsive movement made her finger curl and hook into the first forcep in the row. The whole lot slid out of the cupboard to fall clattering to the floor in a cascade of gleaming chrome.

'My good girl, what on earth are you doing?' A tall woman in a dark-blue dress, with a frosting of white at the collar and cuffs, swept forward crossly, and bent to pick up the fallen instruments just as Bridget, with really shaking hands now, bent to do the same. She scrabbled among the forceps, trying to collect as many as she could, and only succeeded in dropping all those she picked up, so that the tall woman, with a cluck of impatience said sharply, 'Do leave them – I'll pick them up,' which she proceeded to do with deft fingers. Then she hung them back in place and turned to Bridget, who was now standing in dejection behind her.

'I'm so sorry,' Bridget muttered. 'So sorry. I was too early – I thought I'd look about – so sorry – I didn't mean to – '

'Well, no harm done,' the tall woman said briskly. 'Just remember in future that these are valuable pieces of equipment and need to be handled with respect. Clumsy nurses are bad nurses – we must teach you to be more careful, mustn't we?'

'Yes,' Bridget said miserably.

'Yes, Sister,' the tall woman said. 'In hospital, we address people with a particular courtesy.'

3

'Yes, Sister,' Bridget said again, now very near to tears, wishing she could turn and run.

The tall woman seemed to sense her misery, and smiled, a smile that lifted her rather craggy face into softer lines.

'Dear me, but this is an unfortunate beginning for you! But don't worry about it – we all had to start once, and we were all just as nervous as you are!' And Bridget, managing a shaky smile in response, tried to imagine this very masterful woman being as nervous as she was now, and couldn't.

'Well, since you are here early, we'll make the most of the time, and get you sorted out before the others arrive. Come along to my office, now – and you'd better bring your case and leave it in the hall until Margaret shows you your room.'

Bridget picked up the big case and hurried after the tall woman, who was leading the way out across the hall towards a door on the other side of it.

'Have you lunched?'

'Yes, thank you – Sister,' Bridget lied. She hadn't been able to eat for the last two days, so nervous about it all had she been.

'Good – now, leave your luggage there, and come along in.'

Bridget obediently followed her into the office, and sat down in the chair the other woman indicated with a nod of her head, and clasping her hands on her lap, to hide their shaking, waited for what was to come next.

'Now, my dear, let us introduce ourselves to each other. I am Sister Chessman, your Sister Tutor. I will be looking after your tuition here at the Royal for the next three years, and I hope we will be able to be of help to each other. I will do all I can to make a nurse of you, someone of whom the Royal and the profession can be proud, and with interest and intelligent co-operation from you, we should have a

4

very successful and happy three years together.' She leafed through a pile of papers on the desk between them. 'Now, what is your name?'

'Bridget Preston, Sister.'

'Preston – Preston – ah, yes. Here we are.' She pulled one of the sheets of paper out and peered at it. 'I see that you did not come to the Royal for a preliminary interview, because your home is in the North – so we know very little about you. Let me see. You are nineteen?'

Bridget nodded.

'And you have no parents, I see. I'm sorry about that, my dear,' and the all too familiar and hateful look of pity appeared on the craggy face.

'They died when I was a baby,' Bridget began the usual explanation with a spurious ease born of long practice. 'My grandmother brought me up.' She began to stumble a little then. 'She – she died last month – I have a guardian now.'

'I'm sorry,' Sister Chessman said again.

'Well, to tell the truth, she was very old, and I didn't see a lot of her,' Bridget said with a rush of honesty. 'I've been at boarding-school most of my life – I only lived with Grandmother these last two years, and she was pretty much of an invalid – I can't pretend to miss her very much.'

Sister Chessman nodded, looking at the girl in front of her with shrewd but friendly eyes. 'You have had rather a lonely time lately, then?'

Bridget thought of the last two years, the interminable hours in the dingy, big house in the depths of Yorkshire, the hours spent doing such small household tasks as her grandmother's dour housekeeper had allowed her to do, the hours of reading through the ancient collection of dreary books, of solitary walks across the bleak moors, the emptiness that had been her life. But she made no attempt to explain all this. She just nodded.

5

'Why did you decide to be a nurse, Miss Preston? What attracted you to the profession?'

Bridget bit her lip momentarily. How could she explain that to this severe, self-assured woman? Explain the look of rather impatient benevolence on the face of Mr Lessiter, the solicitor her grandmother had appointed as her guardian, when he had come to collect her from her grandmother's house the day after the funeral?

'Well, Bridget, my dear,' he had said briskly, as they sat in the train that carried them both towards the Lessiter home in Edinburgh. 'And what are you going to do now? I'm afraid you'll have to take some sort of job, you know. Your grandmother's income died with her – it was an annuity – and the sale of the house will just about cover the expenses of her illness and funeral and the legacy she left to her housekeeper. Much as Mrs Lessiter and I would like to support you, we aren't in any position to do so unless you make some contribution yourself – '

Bridget had understood the situation at the Lessiter's very quickly, almost before she had been in the house an hour. Mr Lessiter was a busy man, much too occupied with his work to care to have a girl like Bridget cluttering up his life, and Mrs Lessiter, childless as the couple were, had filled her life with her job as an advertising executive, and had no more relish for her unwanted task as joint guardian to Bridget than had her husband.

It had been Bridget herself who had solved the problem. She had remembered the rather nice girl who had come to the house to nurse her grandmother during the last week of her life, the little she had heard from her about being a nurse, and had decided, on the basis of this flimsy knowledge that she, too, would be a nurse.

She had said to the Lessiters, with some diffidence,

that she would like to work in a hospital, and the patent relief on their faces, the warm pleasure with which they had greeted this suggestion, had made it clear to her that she had been right.

'An excellent plan,' Mr Lessiter had said, almost with gaiety. 'Excellent; you'll be far more comfortable living in a Nurses' Home with a lot of girls your own age than with a pair of old fogies like us, eh Elizabeth?' and his wife had smiled back at him and agreed heartily.

Now, Bridget tried to answer Sister Chessman's question with some honesty.

'I – it seemed the best thing to do,' was all she managed.

'Do you know anything about nursing?'

'Well – no, not very much. But I liked science at school – I got quite good O levels in it – though I got A levels in English – '

'Your educational qualifications are quite satisfactory – we have a record of all that here on your application form. No, I want to know *why* you chose nursing. Do you like people? Want to help them?'

'I – I think so, Sister.' Bridget tried again. 'I – I haven't seen much of people, really, not since I left school, and even then, it was a very small school – I didn't get about much. I just worked.'

Somehow, at school, she had never been very good at making friends. The other girls had been so full of their home doings, chatter about their parents, their brothers and sisters, their friends with whom they spent their holidays, that Bridget, lacking these subjects of conversation, had retreated into a quiet, bookish world of her own, a safe world, free from any emotional tangles of the sort other girls seemed to get into. No boy-friends, no violent crushes on other girls at school had ever disturbed the even tenor of her life.

Mercifully, Sister Chessman seemed to understand some of her difficulty in explaining, and said no more

7

about the matter. She busied herself with asking rather more practical questions, about her health, explaining that she would be having a general physical examination by one of the hospital physicians, to make sure she was physically fit for the arduous job of nursing, telling her that she would spend the next three months in the Preliminary Training School, visiting the hospital's wards one day a week, and that if she studied hard, and passed the examination that would be set at the end of that three months, she would be admitted to the Royal as a full student nurse.

'And looking at your scholastic record, I would say you should have little difficulty in coping with your studies, as long as you work hard and don't slack the weeks away. Now, I rather think I hear some of the other girls arriving. If you go to the hall, Margaret, the maid, will show you to your room, and you can unpack. You will have to share a room with other girls while you are here in the Preliminary Training School, I'm afraid – we are very short of single rooms in this building, but later, when you move to the Nurses' Home proper, you will, of course, have a room to yourself. Off you go now, and ask Margaret to send the next arrival in five minutes – I must sort these papers out first.'

Obediently, Bridget turned to go, and was called back just as she reached the door.

'I hope you will be happy with us, Nurse Preston. It will all seem very strange at first, I know, and probably frightening. But we at the Royal understand that, and we want to help. Don't be afraid to come to me if you have any problems. I don't bite – and I do care a great deal about the happiness of every girl in the training school. An unhappy girl makes a bad nurse, and we want you to be a good nurse, as well as a happy person. Remember that, won't you?' She smiled her transforming smile again. 'Welcome to the Royal, Nurse Preston. We are happy to have you with us.'

And with a sudden uprush of emotion Bridget could only smile shakily and nod, before escaping to the hall outside.

There were about half a dozen girls in the hall, none of them with parents accompanying them, yet Bridget felt her heart fail her for a moment. She was so bad at making friends, so unable to chatter easily to strangers, as these girls clearly could. They were talking together as though they had known each other all their lives, heads together, leaning against the radiators in the hall in relaxed attitudes that Bridget envied heartily.

The maid came across the hall as Bridget closed the office door behind her.

'Please, Margaret,' she said. 'Sister Chessman said would you send the next one in to her in five minutes?'

The maid nodded, and one of the girls leaning against the radiator detached herself from the group and came over to Bridget, who was standing a little helplessly next to her suitcase.

'What's she like?' the girl asked.

Bridget looked up at her, a girl taller than herself by a couple of inches, with thick fair hair that curled becomingly into a springing bob round a pointed face, large blue eyes, well made up to show the thick brown lashes to advantage. She had a smooth skin, clear of any blemish, and a neat figure that was perhaps a little too well displayed in a tightly fitting jersey suit. Her legs were long and beautiful, and she wore high-heeled, very fashionable shoes that made Bridget painfully aware of her own sensible Yorkshire brogues.

'I – I beg your pardon?' she said awkwardly.

'What's she like?' the girl said again. 'The old she-dragon in there? Is she a real old battle-axe, or one of those nice motherly types you can push around?'

'She's very – nice, I think,' Bridget said. 'I mean, I

hardly know – I've only been with her a little while – She's a bit – a bit scary, really, I suppose.'

The girl nodded, resignedly. 'I get you. Battle-axe.' She turned to the others.

'We're out of luck,' she announced to them. 'She seems to have scared the pants off this one, anyway.' She turned back to Bridget. 'Who're you? I'm Roberta Aston – Bobby to my friends. And this is Judith Mayer – that tall one with the red hair over there, and this dolly face with all the black hair is Liz Cooper, and that's Dorothy – Jackson, isn't it?' – a quiet-looking girl in a blue coat nodded shortly – 'and this is Mary Byrne, and this is Jean McDonald. I gather from the maid there're four more to come yet. Not exactly a big class, is it? Who're you?'

'Bridget Preston – er, how do you do?'

'And how do *you* do?' Bobby said gaily. 'Look, Margaret says we can share out the rooms how we like – there's one four-bedder, and Liz and Judith and me have already opted to share – and you can join us if you like. You look nice and quiet – do you snore?'

'I don't think so.' Bridget stared fascinatedly at this elegant and loquacious girl, who already seemed to have the whole place organised. 'Have you been here before?' she asked tentatively. The dark girl called Liz moved lazily away from the radiator towards them and laughed huskily.

'Not a bit of it, Bridget,' she said, with an amused note in her voice. 'I've met this type before. Give her five minutes in a place, and she knows it all – who to get things out of, who to avoid, the back way out, and the secret ways in, all the useful things like that.'

Bobby grinned complacently. 'Got it in one, ducky,' she said. 'If you don't look after yourself in this wicked world, no one's going to look after you – take it from one who knows and' as suffered sumfin' crool,' and she

10

struck a mock heroic pose that made them all, including Bridget, laugh.

There was a faint sound from beyond the closed door of Sister Chessman's office, and the maid nodded at the quiet girl called Dorothy, and opened the door for her to go in.

'I'll show you others your rooms, then,' she said. 'And mind you don't make too much noise, or Sister Chessman'll be after you. Come on –'

As Bridget followed the maid and the other girls up the wide, polished, wooden stairs to the bedrooms above, she felt a little better. This gay girl, this Bobby who seemed so self-assured, who had all the qualities that Bridget herself lacked but longed to have, she seemed to like Bridget already, certainly enough to let her share a room with her and the other two girls she had chosen to be her friends. Perhaps life at the Royal wouldn't be too bad, after all. Above all, she reminded herself, as she dropped her suitcase on to one of the beds in the big room Margaret showed them into, above all, it was safe. There was nowhere else to go. The Lessiters didn't really have room for her in their lives, and there was no one else to help her, she told herself practically, but without self-pity. The Royal, or a hospital just like it, was the only answer. It might as well be the Royal as anywhere else.

So, lifting her chin with an effort, she turned to look at the other three girls and the room she was to share with them for the next three months.

Chapter 2

Bridget spent the next weeks in a state of startled happiness that left her almost physically breathless when she thought about it. Everything about her new life was so enjoyable – the lectures were interesting, and with the habit of study and reading she had developed during her schooldays, presented little difficulty. In a way, the ease with which she coped with her work enhanced the greatest pleasure of all – her friendship with the other three girls with whom she shared a room. In the area of study and work, she was superior to them, and in only this. They were gay – particularly Bobby – they had a brand of high spirits that spilled over into their everyday speech and seemed to the hitherto lonely Bridget to be sparkling wit, and they were so pretty.

It was wonderful, Bridget thought, to be like that, admiring these qualities in them without envy. But despite her wholehearted pleasure in their company, her genuine lack of envy, it was equally wonderful to be able to answer any question that Sister Chessman threw at the class, wonderful to sail through a test paper and sit back with the feeling of having produced well-written answers while the others breathed heavily over their pens, and muttered at each other about the hellishness of study.

Liz and Judith, and particularly Bobby, rapidly discovered that Bridget found the work easy, and seized on this ability in her to make their own lives easier. Bobby told Bridget gaily that it was uneconomic, to

13

say the least, for all of them to wear their delicate brains out with work, when she could do it for them. And Bridget, delightedly, agreed. At first, she took her careful lecture notes, made her clear diagrams, and handed over her notebooks after lectures so that the others could copy them at their leisure, while they sat in class and passed silly notes to each other, giggling softly, and looking at Sister Chessman with limpid innocence in their eyes when she caught sight of them in the back row obviously not working at all. By the end of the second week they found an even easier way of keeping their notes up to date. They just handed their books over to the willing Bridget who would copy her own notes into them. Bridget didn't mind in the least, for not only was she helping her friends – she found it helped her to learn her work very quickly. By the time she had written out the notes four times, made four sets of diagrams, she knew the material backwards.

There was only one aspect of their life in the Preliminary Training School that worried her, only one in which the other three were better than she was. This showed on the day each week when the eleven students, awkward in the white coats that the PTS students wore, were shepherded over to the hospital to spend time in the wards.

On the first of these days, Bridget, together with Bobby and Liz, was sent to the male surgical ward. She stood at the door of the big ward, her heart beating thickly, her face white under its dusting of freckles, feeling her knees shake. How could she face a ward full of men, ill men? She knew there were thirty of them, that the long ward held fifteen beds on each side, and she dreaded the thought of having to walk down that ward, with thirty pairs of eyes fixed on her. But Bobby and Liz had no such fears.

'Cor!' Bobby said in her mock cockney accent. 'Cor – Thirty lovely men – just think of it!' And she tightened her white belt around her slender waist, shook her fair hair into an even more becoming casualness, and walked into the ward, with Liz beside her, her slender hips waggling in very conscious provocation, the frightened Bridget scuttling shyly in their shadow.

Sister was at the far end of the ward, standing beside a bed, as the three students walked towards her, and her round young face creased into a faint frown as she heard the decided wolf whistle one of the patients produced at the sight of the beautiful Bobby, walking down the ward with her fair hair swinging, her big eyes fixed on Sister's face with apparent unawareness of the stir she was creating among the patients.

But Sister was young enough, and had a sufficiently satisfying private life of her own, to lack the vindictive jealousy of a young pretty student some of the other Sisters at the Royal occasionally displayed, and contented herself with a wry comment on the length of Bobby's hair, advising her that she would have to have it cut or wear it up before she came to this ward again. And Bobby demurely agreed, knowing full well that she looked as good with her hair piled on her head as with it swinging loose round her ears.

Bobby and Bridget were sent to give drinks of hot milk and cocoa to the men, while Liz, much to her disgust, was taken by Sister on a tedious tour of the ward cupboards. Her only comfort was that Bobby and Bridget would have to do this on the next visit, while she would be able to talk to the patients.

By the time the two girls had loaded the trolley with cups and saucers and the jugs of drinks, Bridget felt a little better. She had something to do, and perhaps the business of pouring the drinks would make it possible to avoid the men's eyes as they went round.

'You pour, I'll dish 'em out,' Bobby said quickly, as they rattled their way out of the kitchen into the big

15

ward. And Bridget was only too glad to agree. Industriously she filled the cups with steaming milk, while Bobby happily tripped from trolley to bed and back again, giggling at the men, joining in with their chatter, and generally enjoying herself while producing a very enjoyable performance for the delighted patients. Sister was out of earshot with Liz, the staff nurse was occupied in a corner with a tricky dressing, and the other nurses who belonged to the ward had gone off to drink their own morning coffee. Bobby had the field to herself, and made the most of it.

But just before they had finished the round, when Bobby was standing by the trolley, holding her hand out to Bridget for the next cup Sister appeared at the ward door with Liz in tow. And at this same moment, one of the up-patients passed by the trolley, a young man with a plaster cast on one arm, and he pinched Bobby's bottom as he shuffled by. Bobby yelped with a mixture of surprise and pleasure, throwing out one arm. Bridget, nervous and startled, lurched backwards, and a jug of hot milk went splashing messily all over the polished floor, sent there by her flying hand.

'Oh, for heaven's sake, you stupid girl!' Sister bore down on Bridget with rage all over her face. 'This floor was polished this morning, and now look at it! How clumsy can you get! Go and get a mop from the kitchen at once and clean it up, go along now! And you – ' she turned to Bobby. 'Even if you were splashed with hot milk, there was no need to make a noise like that! Are you scalded?'

And Bobby, with a sharp glance at the flaming-faced and miserable Bridget said, 'Er – no, Sister, thank you – I'll help Nurse Preston, shall I?'

'You'll do nothing of the sort. She was stupid enough to make the mess, she can clear it up. You come with me, and Nurse Preston – hurry up with clearing that mess you've made!' And she sailed off down the

16

ward, with Liz and Bobby behind her. Bobby cast an apologetic look over her shoulder at Bridget, standing mortified with shame and a sort of helpless rage, in a pool of slimy hot milk, and shrugged slightly.

Bridget spent a dreadful half-hour on her knees, mopping up milk and re-applying the polish the spill had removed. The obvious sympathy of the men made her feel worse. Even when the boy who had started it all by pinching Bobby's bottom came over to tell her how sorry he was, that it hadn't been her fault, she kept her head down, refusing to look up or answer him, so that he shrugged and went away, leaving her to her shame and misery.

Later that day, when the four girls reassembled in their bedroom, Bobby had the grace to apologise to Bridget.

'I am sorry, Bridie, love, truly I am – ' she said winningly. 'But I couldn't tell that Sister it was me that spilt the milk, could I? If I had, I'd have had to tell her that boy started it by getting fresh, and then she'd have given the boy hell, and we're supposed to look after the patients, aren't we? It wouldn't be good nursing to shop a patient, now would it?' And Bridget, though she was still smarting a little from the episode, found herself laughing, completely disarmed, as usual, by Bobby's undoubted charm. They spent the evening in a visit to a local cinema, and Bridget tried to forget the whole business, only grateful it would be another six days before she would have to face a ward again.

Unfortunately for Bridget, however, the episode had been reported to Sister Chessman, not because the Ward Sister was still particularly annoyed about it – her temper, while hot, cooled rapidly – but because it was usual practice to report fully on each student that came to the wards from the PTS. And Sister Chessman made a mental note that this girl Preston would bear watching. As she told Matron, on her weekly visit to the lady's office to report on the progress of the school, 'I'm a little doubtful about Nurse Preston. Her background isn't all it might be – these quiet girls of strict upbringing tend to run wild when they get to hospital, in my experience. And she spends her time with three very giddy people.'

'Are you worried about the other three, too, then?' Matron asked.

And Sister Chessman, frowning a little, said slowly, 'I'm not sure. They have very high spirits, but they are the sort that can be guided. I think. I much prefer high spirits to this quietness – you just don't know where you are with Nurse Preston. She doesn't talk to me very much, though the others chatter away freely enough. I could be being unfair – maybe she was just clumsy from nervousness, though Sister on the ward thought she was making a scene for attention's sake.' Altogether, it was unfortunate for Bridget that the Ward Sister was as young as she was. An older, more experienced, woman would have recognised that Bridget was nervous, not an attention seeker.

As the weeks wore on, Bridget got to know a little more about her new friends. They showed little interest in her background, though Liz once or twice asked her about the sort of life she had led before coming to the Royal. But Bridget had shrugged her questions away, and Liz didn't persist. But they talked about themselves a good deal, and Bridget listened fascinatedly, particularly to Bobby.

She was the only daughter of fairly rich parents, and as far as Bridget could tell, had never had to ask more than once for anything she wanted. Bridget got the impression that her parents had little time for their only child, regarding her with a sort of impatient affection, discharging all their parental duties by spending money. There had been nannies, expensive boarding-schools – several, for Bobby admitted unashamedly to being

18

expelled from one after the other – foreign holidays, gay Mediterranean cruises. And Bobby liked her life as it was very much. She had come to the Royal because she wanted to live in London on her own, and somewhat to her surprise and chagrin, her father had balked at her demand for an allowance to run a flat of her own. He had told her that she either had to live at home in Surrey, or get a job living-in where she would be supervised. And as Bobby said with a grimace, 'That meant nursing. So here I am.'

Judith, the one of the three Bridget found least approachable, for all her surface gaiety, was the daughter, surprisingly, of a parson in a market town in the Midlands. She too, Bridget discovered, wanted to get to London, and the only way she could do it was by nursing – and as she said smoothly. 'The parents think it's a "Good" thing to do – service to others and all that guff. My God, but it's good to get away from that bloody vicarage – ' and Bridget had felt chilled at the coldness, the calculation of her.

Liz, too, seemed to find Judith's attitude to her parents rather distasteful. Her own parents were apparently happy, friendly people with a shop in a country town in Devonshire, and they had been delighted when their daughter had decided to become a nurse.

'They're not too well off,' she explained, almost apologetically. 'This way, I earn my own living, and get a career as well – they think it's a great idea. And with two sisters younger than me, they've got a lot of expenses –' and Bridget had smiled at her across the room, and poured out another cup of coffee for her, feeling a warmth for this pretty, friendly girl, who seemed so normal, somehow, the one of the three somehow most like Bridget herself.

It was about half-way through the three months in the PTS that Bobby at last made the contact with the medical staff she wanted. As she had said firmly one evening, when the four girls were sitting in their room over cups of coffee made on the gas-ring each room was provided with, 'Life in this hospital will be pretty drear if we don't get to know some of the men around the place.'

'The patients?' Bridget asked, remembering the boy who had pinched Bobby's round bottom.

'Not on your life, my pretty,' Bobby had said, stretching catlike on her bed, and grinning across at Bridget. 'I mean *real* men. I mean, what are we here for?'

Judith chuckled fatly from her own heap of pillows. 'I know what I'm here for,' she said, peering into the mirror she was holding as she combed her thick red hair into a sleek style. 'I want to get married as fast as ever I can. And not just to anyone. I want a man who can keep me in the style to which I have every intention of becoming accustomed as fast as ever I can.'

And Liz, from across the room agreed. 'A nice handsome doctor with prospects and a private income if it's at all possible,' she said dreamily. 'Someone who will think I'm God's gift to doctorkind, who'll devote all the time when he isn't saving lives to my special welfare. There ought to be a few of 'em around a hospital this size to choose from.'

'Oh,' said Bridget, startled. 'I – I hadn't thought of that.'

Bobby sat up and stared at her. 'Come off it, little one! I mean, I know you *look* like a schoolgirl, and behave a bit like one sometimes, but surely you aren't really as green as that! Don't you want a man of your own, or are you odd or something?'

'I – I'm not odd, of course I'm not,' Bridget said hastily. 'I – well, I just hadn't thought about it, I suppose.'

'Well, it's time you did, sweetie,' Judith said. 'Why on earth come to work in a hospital, for God's sake, if not for the – social opportunities? Don't tell me you're like that dreary Dorothy Jackson, all religion and a burning vocation to help suffering mankind, and all that rubbish.'

'Of course I'm not!' Bridget said indignantly. She, too, found Dorothy Jackson, with her sanctimonious voice, her tendency to smarm round Sister Chessman, and her self-righteous and very obvious departure for Church each Sunday, unpleasant. 'It's just that I hadn't thought – I hadn't thought about – getting married,' and her voice faltered on the words. Indeed, she never had thought about marriage. She hadn't even thought about having boy-friends. She had never had the opportunity to meet any boys of her own age, and so found men rather frightening people. The thought of having boy-friends of her own, of ever getting close enough to a man to even think of marriage made her boggle.

Bobby laughed softly. 'We'll have to take you in hand, Bridie, my pretty, 'deed and 'deed we will! You're not bad looking, and with the right clothes and a bit of know-how you'll go a long way.'

'I haven't got much in the way of clothes.' Bridget found the thought of being dressed in the sort of clothes the others wore decidedly attractive suddenly, despite her fear of men, her diffidence towards the idea of marriage.

'All for one and one for all!' Liz said gaily. 'You do our notes for us, and the least we can do is show you how to dress and lend you some gear – ' and Bridget smiled gratefully at her. Of all the three, Liz was certainly the most appreciative of Bridget's help with their work, and had an easy generosity of nature that was extremely appealing.

So, when a few weeks after this conversation, Bobby came bursting into the PTS sitting-room with triumph all over her face, Bridget knew what was coming.

21

'I've done it, I've done it, I've done it!' she cried.

'Don't tell me, let me guess!' Liz looked up from the pair of stockings she was darning. 'The most famous surgeon in the place has just fallen on his knees at the sight of your gorgeous orbs, and begged you to take him and his little all for ever and a day!'

Dorothy Jackson, sitting in lonely state at the other side of the room, with text-books spread ostentatiously all round her, sighed loudly, and collecting her equipment, left the room to the four friends, disapproval written all over her straight back as she went. Bobby stuck her tongue out at the slam of the door behind her, and then jumped gaily on to an armchair. 'Listen, you lucky, lucky people. Your Auntie Bobby, who has the welfare of each and every one of you dear creatures firmly ensconced in her kind heart has made a social arrangement for you. Say thank you nicely.'

'Thank you nicely,' said Judith promptly. 'What is it?'

'*Well*,' said Bobby, with theatrical emphasis. 'I was just walking quietly across the hospital courtyard on the way back from that nice little errand Sister Chessman sent me on, and what should come across the said yard but the most *beautiful* piece of man I have ever clapped these young eyes of mine upon. To put it in a nutshell, and without any vulgarity, he was gorgeous!'

'So?' Liz was getting impatient.

'So,' Bobby said. 'I, without a moment's hesitation, and knowing full well that you three dear souls were sitting here positively languishing for the company of a few males, did my famous imitation of a lady tripping over a stone. And the gorgeous object caught me! Never even noticed there wasn't a stone there! Cor, but I'm a talented creature – admit it!'

'We admit it.' Liz was nearly bouncing with impatience. 'So what happened?'

'So we're all invited to a hospital party tonight as ever

22

is! Doctors' common-room, nine o'clock sharp, in your best bibs and tuckers! How's that then!'

'All of us!' Judith said. 'All four of us?'

'Sure!' Bobby said. 'He wanted to go and buy me some coffee in the canteen, to get me over the shock of my fall, you see – ' She smirked wickedly. 'And I told him I had to get back to the kind care of Sister Chessman, or I would have loved to drink coffee with him – you know, a delicate mixture of interest and maidenly modesty. It always gets 'em. Anyway, he said in that case, come and have something a bit stronger by way of restorative tonight, so *I* said – more maidenly modesty, and general nice mindedness – that I had three very nice friends over here in the schoolroom without whom I couldn't *possibly* go anywhere, so he said, with charming promptness, Bring 'em along!' She giggled, her eyes sparkling very attractively. 'He said if they were half as nice as me, they'd be very ornamental about the old common-room, so I assured him you were all much *much* nicer! Cor, was I modest today! The strain is killing me!'

'But so late!' Bridget felt fear rising in her as she thought of herself going to a party. 'We can't possibly go – we have to be in here at ten o'clock – you know they lock up then!'

'Bridie, Bridie, dear!' Bobby cooed across at her. 'Be your age, my little one. A couple of bob in Margaret's outstretched palm, and the back door will be ever so conveniently forgotten tonight – and even if it isn't, I'm a dead ringer at climbing into first-floor windows up fire escapes. Let's live dangerously, girl! Fear you not, we'll get in again! It's the least of our problems.'

Amid the general hilarity of the other three, Bridget was silenced. She was definitely afraid, mostly of the thought of going to a party where there would be lots of people she didn't know, partly because of the fear of being caught out of the building after the curfew

23

set by Sister Chessman. But she said no more about her feelings, for she knew that Bobby's high good humour could rapidly deteriorate into irritation, and she had no intention of upsetting Bobby. Bobby happy was a wonderful and exciting person to be with, and could make them all feel marvellous. But Bobby in a bad mood could plunge them all into gloom and despondency, so strong was her effect on them.

So, at eight o'clock that night, she let the other three lend her clothes, let them show her how to put on some make-up, let the clever Liz comb her hair into a very becoming new shape, and said not a word about her nervousness. When they had finished with her, she stared in the mirror at the new Bridget, and at what she saw there found a sort of excited pleasure battling with her apprehension.

Her thick dark-brown hair was swept on each side of her face into gleaming wings, the ends turning up slightly so that the light caught the tips with a gleam of gold. The big, grey eyes under fine-winged eyebrows looked deeper and somehow larger, thanks to the smudge of eye-shadow Liz had expertly applied to the lids and the touch of mascara on the lashes. Even her freckles, something she had always disliked on herself, looked different, attractive somehow, dusting her nose and cheeks above the soft, rose-coloured lipstick Liz had found for her. She was wearing one of Judith's dresses, a deep green one that fitted her well, showing her long waist and pretty tilted bust to perfection.

'Oh,' she breathed softly, as she stared at herself, and impulsively, Liz hugged her. 'I look quite – nice,' Bridget said wonderingly.

'Of course you do, mouse!' Liz said affectionately. 'You've got lots of potential. You've just got to learn how to develop it, that's all! You're as nice to look at as the next person – and don't you forget it! If you feel pretty, then you'll *look* pretty – it never fails. You'll have lots of fun tonight – come on.'

And with pleasurable anticipation at last overcoming her nervousness, Bridget 'came on', and followed her three friends as they slipped silently down the wide staircase towards the back door. Bridget was going to her first party, with her first real friends, and Bridget was a very happy girl indeed.

Chapter 3

Bridget had never seen so many people crushed into one room before. It was not a big room, either, as far as she could see through the crowd and the dim light and the thick drift of tobacco smoke that clung to the ceiling and sent tendrils down among the close-packed bodies beneath. She was still feeling bewildered. When they had walked into the doctors' common-room, Bridget hiding behind Judith, they had been greeted with a boisterous shout from a tall man who had been busily working with bottles and glasses in one corner.

'Hallo! – Then you managed to escape from your wardress? Well done! Clive, David, Ken – meet some of the new lambs!' and he had taken Bobby's hand, thrown one arm across Liz's shoulders, and with Judith and Bridget following, led the four girls towards a group of men who had been leaning against the makeshift bar. There had been introductions, to which the other three girls had made gay response, only Bridget seeming in the least bit shy of these strangers, not that anyone seemed to notice her shyness. Someone had thrust a glass into her hand – the contents of which she had not attempted to taste – and in seconds, Bobby and Judith were dancing, while Liz was chattering to one of the men as though she had known him all her life.

The room filled with people very quickly, one or two of the girls in uniform, some of the men in white coats, and the noise increased in proportion. A record-player ground out raucous music that made Bridget's head

27

swim a little, and people chattered at the tops of their voices in an attempt to make themselves heard above it. But despite the noise, and the smell of smoke, Bridget was enjoying herself.

She sat perched on the arm of a chair, against the wall, and watched the dancers and the chatterers with wide eyes. She was quite happy to be by herself in the middle of it all – indeed, her pleasure would have been diminished if she had not been able to sit quietly and watch, turning her still untasted drink in her hands.

Bobby, twisting merrily in the middle of the room, her fair hair swinging round her flushed cheeks, was a joy to watch, and when one of the other men, with a neat movement, ousted the tall man with whom she had been dancing, taking his place with a mock bow, Bridget chuckled. The tall man, without any apparent annoyance, made his way through the crowded scrap of dance floor towards Bridget's corner, and flopped into the chair whose arm she was occupying.

'Between ourselves, sweetheart,' he said, grinning up at her, 'I'd had about enough of that. Me, I wasn't made for these energetic type of dances. Give me a nice smoochy blues any day. What say you?'

'I – er – I don't really know,' Bridget said awkwardly. 'I've never done much dancing – '

'No? We'll have to remedy that!' He leaned forwards, and pulled her round to look at him. 'Now, which one are you? You *are* one of the new lambs, aren't you? Didn't you come in with Bobby and the others?'

'Yes – ' Bridget looked at him properly for the first time. He had a square face, with deep clefts in each cheek, clefts that had obviously started out as dimples when he had been a child, a wide, friendly mouth with very even white teeth, brown eyes that were crinkled with laughter-lines under slightly untidy eyebrows, and crisp dark-brown hair that was cut close to a well-shaped head.

28

'I seem to have missed out on the introductions,' he said, his smile deepening as he noticed the ready colour climb into her cheeks. 'I'm Josh Simpson. My misguided parents named me after a rather dull Biblical type, but try not to hold it against me. Anyway, Joshua will be an excellent name for me when I get my knighthood, don't you think? Sir Joshua Simpson, don't you know – surgeon extraordinary to the Queen – very extraordinary!' And he struck a heroic pose that made Bridget gurgle with laughter.

'I'm Bridget Preston,' she said, in response to his questioning face. 'And I did come with Bobby and the others. It – it was very nice of you to ask us.'

He stood up, and smiled down at her. 'But I *am* nice – very nice. Nicest man in this here mess of men, believe me. Come on – let's find a nice smoochy blues record, and try you out on that – ' and he pulled her to her feet, took her glass from her hand to put it down on the cluttered bar, and dragged her behind him to the record-player in the corner.

'Here you are,' he said, rapidly scrabbling through the untidy pile of records. 'Here's a gorgeous one – ' and he put it on the turn-table, and led her to the middle of the room.

As the other couples, some with loud shouts of disagreement at Josh's choice of music, moved towards each other to dance, and others, only interested in the fast, twisting records, made their way towards the drinks, Josh put his arms round Bridget, and started to dance. She had only ever danced with girls at school before, but she had a natural sense of rhythm, and despite her nervousness, the music soon relaxed her, and she found herself moving smoothly, matching her steps to his.

'That's better.' His voice came very close to her ear. 'Relax and enjoy it! Come on, now – ' and his arms tightened round her, and she felt his cheek against her hair, could feel his breath warm on her skin. For a moment she resisted the closeness, but then as the music swelled, and slid into a more definite beat, she did indeed relax, and danced as she had never danced before.

It was odd, the way she was able to anticipate each move he made, the way her feet seemed automatically to go the right way, the comfort she found in his firm clasp. She danced on, eyes half closed, the soft wail of the trumpet in the music sending a delicious sleepiness through her, a sleepiness that in no way altered her pleasure in the dance. When the music stopped, she stood surprised for a moment, still held closely by Josh's strong arms, before suddenly feeling all her shyness come surging back, so that she pulled herself awkwardly from his arms, and stood blinking at him.

'Th – thank you – that was fun – ' she managed, and he laughed at her obvious confusion.

'Bless the child, but she's a shrinking-type violet! Are you really as shy as you seem to be?'

She bit her lip. 'I'm sorry,' she said. 'I – I've never – well, I'm not really used to parties. I am sorry.'

'Don't apologise, my pretty!' He touched her face then, gently running his finger down the curve of her cheek. 'Believe me, sweetheart, you make a more than refreshing change. I'd forgotten there were girls in the world like you. I only ever meet the other kind. Come on – let's have a drink, and find a nice cosy corner, and you can tell me the story of your life – '

As he pulled her towards the bar again, she caught a glimpse of Bobby and Liz and Judith across the room. Almost to her horror, she saw that Judith was sitting perched on one man's lap, while Bobby was busily parrying the attentions of a man who, even to Bridget's inexperienced eyes, seemed to be rather full of drink.

'You see what I mean?' Josh's voice came from above her, and she turned startled eyes on to his face. 'Shy girls are at a premium these days – ' and he, too, looked across at the others, but without any of the shocked surprise on his face that Bridget had felt. 'Not that those friends of yours aren't crackers – gorgeous types, hmm? Can't say I blame David.'

'David?' Bridget asked, as they arrived at the bar, and Josh began to mix drinks for them both, more to say something than because she really wanted to know which one David was.

'David is the one who's working so hard with your Bobby,' Josh said over his shoulder. 'Tell me, how far will he get with her, do you suppose?'

Bridget, for all her inexperience, was not completely ignorant, and as she saw David make an even more determined lunge at Bobby, this time succeeding in kissing her very thoroughly, a success that she could see Bobby did not object to with any real strength, she blushed scarlet.

'I – I really don't know,' she said stiffly, and Josh, the drinks now ready, turned and looked across the room too.

'Whoops! My money's on David, lucky dog!' he said, laughing. 'That's some girl.'

'She's very nice!' Bridget was suddenly angry with this handsome, tall man beside her. 'She can't help it if – some drunken – drunken ass makes a nuisance of himself!'

He looked at her, and his face softened. 'I'm sorry, Bridget. I didn't mean to be rude about your friend. I'm sure she's a very nice girl – '

'Oh, course she is!' Bridget said hotly. 'She can't help it if she's so pretty people make a fuss of her, can she?'

'I suppose not – ' Then he laughed again. 'Come on – let's find a corner somewhere and wrap ourselves round these highly restorative-type medicines, and you can prove to me just how shy you really are – '

And obediently, Bridget followed, still smarting slightly about his implied criticism of Bobby, but attracted to him far too much to willingly abandon his company.

They settled themselves on a corner of a couch, and Josh put a glass in her hand, and looking at her over the top of his, said softly, 'Skol!' and Bridget, unable to refuse the drink, smiled stiffly back and said, 'Skol!' too, swallowing a mouthful of the cold, sweetish mixture he had given her.

'Come on, now,' he said, his face serious for the first time. 'I truly would like to know about you. Are you as shy as you seem? Or is it a pretty pose? My instincts tell me it's the real McCoy. Let me guess, hmm? Straight from school, and loving parents, and never been out on your own before.'

Bridget, suddenly not caring about the possibility of pity said, 'I left school a couple of years ago – I'm nineteen, you know – '

'Honestly?' He looked genuinely surprised. 'I'd not have given you a minute over seventeen – though that's silly, isn't it? I mean, you have to be eighteen even to start nursing here, don't you?'

Bridget nodded. 'Mmm. And I have no parents. Died when I was a child. I lived with my grandmother till *she* died a couple of months ago.'

There was none of the pity she hated on his face, and for this alone she warmed to him. 'Sounds a dullish sort of life. Was it?'

She took another sip of her drink, and felt the warmth of the gin in it slide into her veins. 'Pretty dull. It's – it's marvellous to be here – to – well, to be on my own. Not that I'm lonely, of course. I've got my friends,' and she said it with a sort of pride that made Josh suddenly feel the pity that she had thought she had managed to avoid – not that Bridget noticed it. She was looking dreamily across the room at the others. 'They are such fun,' she said with a sudden rush of confidence. 'They do all the things I'd like to do – they're marvellous – '

'Don't let them change you too much will you?' Josh, too, looked across at the other girls with their three escorts. 'You're fine as you are, Tiddler.'

She flushed, and with a courage born of the drink she was now steadily swallowing said, 'Why not? You said yourself I was dull.'

'Nothing of the sort!' he said indignantly. 'I just said you'd had a dull life – but *you* aren't dull – not a bit of it! You're sweet – '

And she blushed hotly again at the warmth in his brown eyes, and dropped her own gaze to her glass.

Bobby's voice above them pulled her back from her confusion. 'Help!' she said gaily, flopping into the couch beside them. 'That David's quite a character, Josh! Shouldn't he have a keeper or something? A girl isn't safe with someone like that!'

Josh laughed, and leaning back, threw a negligent arm across Bobby's shoulders. 'He's all right – just gets all excited when he meets gorgeous girls. Can't blame him for that, can you?' And with a return to his mock heroics, he pulled her to him, and held her close.

'What a woman!' he proclaimed, winking at Bridget over Bobby's smooth head. 'Is this the face that launched a thousand ships, the face that set the hearts of every medico for miles around beating with unrequited passion? Woe is us! You'll have us all leaping into sterilisers or something to drown ourselves and our sorrows, you and your luverly big blue eyes!'

Bobby gurgled with pleasure, and said with a pretended severity that convinced no one, 'And don't you start, Buster! Just you be a good doctor and go and get me a drink. I need one.'

He got to his feet with a deep sigh. 'You see?' he said to Bridget. 'One word from this luscious creature and we all run. I go, Madam, I go forthwith,' and with another deep bow, he turned and shoved his way through the mob towards the bar.

'He's nice, isn't he?' Bobby's voice sounded slightly sharp to Bridget, and she turned and looked at her in some surprise.

'Josh? Mmm. Very nice.'

'Well, listen, Bridie, my love. I saw him first, hmm? You know what I mean?'

Bridget stared at Bobby, at the faint line on the smooth brow, and said awkwardly, 'Saw him first? What do you mean, Bobby?'

'Just this, my lovey.' Bobby leaned forward. 'I know you haven't been around much, so you can't be expected to know the rights and wrongs of – shall we say, social behaviour? I saw Josh first, just that. I met him in the courtyard, and if I hadn't, we wouldn't be here tonight. And I like Josh – he's my type. So just hands off, hmm? I'd hate us to spoil a beautiful friendship just because you don't know enough to leave another girl's friends alone – and Josh is *my* friend first. OK?'

Bridget stared at her, her mind whirling with gin and surprise. 'I'm sorry, Bobby – please, don't be cross! I wasn't – wasn't trying to – I mean, I'm not like that, really I'm not!'

Bobby smiled cheerfully then, the faint displeasure on her face that had so chilled Bridget disappeared. 'That's all right then, lovey!' She hugged her briefly. 'I should have known better, shouldn't I? You're a *real* friend – not the sort to pinch another girl's men – sorry I mentioned it – '

'Here you are, beautiful!' Josh reappeared with a glass in his hand. 'Long and cold and full of gin, just like the Chief of Staff's wife! Drink up!' and Bobby took the glass from him, and drank up, smiling brilliantly at Josh over the rim.

When she had finished it, she put the glass on the

34

floor beside her, and stood up, holding her hands out to Josh.

'Can you Madison, Josh?' she asked gaily. 'I've just learnt how, and I'm longing to show off – come and help me – ' and Josh, apparently nothing loth, followed her on to the dancing area to join her in the steps of the Madison, leaving Bridget with a warm smile over his shoulder.

With a smooth ease that Bridget found herself admiring, Bobby collected Liz and Judith and the other three men at the end of the dance, and brought them back to Bridget's corner, managing to arrange them all so that Bridget found herself sitting next to the now rather morose David. But as the evening wore on, he seemed to accept the fact that Bobby was not very interested in him, and turned his attentions to Bridget, who found herself dancing with him several times. She was a bit frightened of him at first, but he made no attempt to treat her as he had treated Bobby earlier in the evening, only holding her close while they danced. Bridget was grateful to him for seeming to realise that she didn't really like being held too close, relaxing his grip on her as soon as she pulled back slightly from him.

Liz and Judith both seemed very happy with their two partners. Liz with the one called Ken, a man as fair as she was dark, seeming particularly happy.

It was past twelve before Bobby made any move to go, when she said with a regretful move in Josh's direction. 'We'd better be moving, Josh. We'll have to climb into the PTS as it is – '

With much hilarity, the four men escorted them across the courtyard towards the PTS building, and with many giggling shushes from Bobby, helped them creep up to the back door, and kept watch for them as they slipped into the dark and silent house. Liz and Bobby were the last two to come in, and Bridget couldn't help noticing the look of smooth pleasure

35

on Bobby's face as she brushed her hand across her smudged lipstick.

Why should I care? she asked herself reasonably, as the four of them silently undressed in their dark bedroom, and slid into their beds. If he wanted to kiss her goodnight, that's their business – and Bobby saw him first –

But she couldn't help caring a little. Josh had seemed to her to be so very nice, so much nicer than David with whom Bridget had spent the end of the evening. But there it was. If he was meant to be Bobby's friend, he was, and that was all there was to it. Bridget fell asleep at last, her mind a confused mêlée of thoughts about Bobby, about her friendship and how much it meant to Bridget, and thoughts about Josh, and how nice it could have been if it had been Bridget who 'had seen him first'.

Chapter 4

The final exams of the PTS came on them suddenly, and for a week, Bobby and Liz and Judith spent every spare moment poring over books, feverishly repeating facts to themselves and groaning because they hadn't worked harder from the beginning. With infinite patience, Bridget helped them, listening to their halting recitals of the various facts they should know – and didn't know – correcting written answers for them, and generally nursing them through the actual week of examinations.

To her own delight and embarrassment, Bridget was second in class when the results came out; only the sanctimonious Dorothy had beaten her to first place. Mary Byrne, a quiet and hard working Irish girl came closely after Bridget in third place, and the rest of the class marks strung out reasonably until the list showed Bobby's, Liz's, and Judith's marks. They had scraped through by the skin of their teeth; indeed, had Judith had one mark less, she would have failed, and that would have been that. Sister Chessman made it quite clear that the Royal had no room for people who couldn't pass their examinations.

But the three of them escaped with nothing worse than a severe reprimand from Sister Chessman, and a strong recommendation to work harder in the future.

Bobby said shrewdly, after they had been released from Sister Chessman's office, 'Not to worry, my beauties. That there old basket is the sort that likes gay people like us. She might tell us off for laziness because it's the right thing to do, but inside, she likes us. I know that.'

Bridget heard this, and felt her heart sink. She too, had realised that Sister Chessman, while scrupulously avoiding any hint of favouritism, preferred the gaiety and charm of her three friends to Bridget's own quietness. She had noticed Sister Chessman looking at her with a sort of baffled irritation on her face when she sat with the class conducting free discussion sessions, sessions during which Bridget had never been able to say a word. Bridget felt, not without just cause, it cannot be denied, that she would have to watch her step where Sister Chessman was concerned.

The very first morning they spent as real students at the Royal came at last, and Bridget sat with the rest of the class at the big round table behind the dining-room door – the one specially reserved for each new intake, and consequently called the Lambing Pen by the rest of the nurses – and shook inside. It had been so strange to wake that morning in a small room of her own, not to see Bobby's crumpled bed across the room, not to hear Judith and Liz muttering as they crawled crossly out of their beds. And then, getting into uniform – that had been odd too. Instead of the white coat she had worn for the past three months, there was a striped dress, with complicated fastenings at the front, an apron that rustled with starch, a cap so stiff that it would hardly stay on her smooth hair, a collar so crisp that already it was reddening the soft skin of her neck. But she had managed to dress at last, and now there she sat in the dining-room, at her first breakfast, watching the big room fill, too nervous to touch the scrambled eggs and toast that were offered, settling for a cup of tea.

It was like an aviary full of blue and white birds, she thought, watching wide-eyed. Some hundred nurses came fluttering into the dining-room, white aprons flapping as they moved, white caps bobbing like crests on black, brown, and red heads, slender, black-stockinged legs twinkling as they carried their breakfasts from the hot plate to the tables. There were some lordly staff nurses with black belts gleaming with silver buckles, caps embellished with lacy bows and strings, who sat in casual elegance while a maid brought their breakfasts to them, the only nurses in the room accorded this privilege.

And the noisc – the rattling of dishes, the high, chattering voices, the hiss of steam from the big boiler that provided hot water for the big teapots, the noise battered against her ears. Somehow, despite her nervousness, her fears about where she would be working, her shrinking dread of the day on the wards ahead of her, Bridget felt suddenly safe, and warm, a sense of belonging in this aviary, for after all, wasn't she as bird-like as the rest of them? And she smoothed her shaking hands across the smooth starch of her apron, under the table, and tried to relax.

Liz grinned at her across the table, seeming to read her thoughts.

'It's a giggle, eh, Bridget?' she said softly. 'I mean, get us! All dolled up like nurses – anyone who didn't know any better'd think we *were* nurses, just to look at us. And if anyone were to faint in front of me, or be sick, or anything, so help me I'd do exactly the same. Are you going to eat that egg? Because if you aren't, hand it over – I'm building up my strength against the horrors that lie ahead,' and she leaned over and scooped Bridget's uneaten meal on to her own plate.

The dining-room slid into silence suddenly, as a blue figure came bustling in and made her way towards a little dais at the end of the room.

'Night Sister,' breathed Bobby softly. 'Come to call the roll and tell us where we're to work.' Night Sister looked sharply across at the junior table and said dryly, 'We do not talk once I arrive to call the roll, Nurses. Remember that, please.' And of course it was Bridget who blushed scarlet as Sister's eye fell on her, while Bobby merely sat and looked the picture of innocence.

The recital of names was quick, each nurse replying with a mumbled, 'Yes, Sister,' and at the end of it, Night Sister read out where various people were to work. To her horror, Bridget found herself allocated to Men's Surgical – which caused the others to make envious faces in her direction – while Bobby was sent to Casualty – she brightened visibly at this – and the other two to women's wards.

In strict order of seniority, the nurses began to leave the dining-room, the lordly staff nurses first, the new class straight from PTS last of all. And Bridget scuttled unhappily in the lee of her classmates, and found all her old misery coming back. How could she face that ward full of men? All her other trips to the hospital from PTS had been to women's wards, and children's wards, apart from that one disastrous afternoon on the male surgical ward, and she wished with all her heart that she could change places with Liz or Judith, both of whom would willingly have changed places with her. But it couldn't be helped, and she arrived at the door of her new ward just behind the last of the senior nurses, and stood in the lobby for a moment, clutching her cape in cold hands, looking around for someone to tell her what to do.

A thin-faced girl in a rather grubby uniform came towards her at last, and said. 'Preston? I'm Barnett – next after you, I was junior pro till this morning, but now you're down among the dregs – and you can have it. Come on – I'm to show you around, and there's one hell of a lot to do before Sister gets here to take the report from the night staff. Come on – shove your cape in the linen cupboard – '

And Bridget followed her into the ward at a trot, her

head down. The ward looked different this morning – not so tidy for one thing. Two of the night nurses were feverishly making beds, one eye on the clock, while the senior night nurse sat at the desk, her cap sideways on her untidy head, scribbling away in the report book for all she was worth. There were men lounging about, some of them very unshaven, others looking fresh and clean as they emerged from the bathroom at the end of the ward. A lackadaisical maid was collecting dirty breakfast dishes from the bed-tables, and a couple of the day nurses were rushing around with screens and trolleys, getting patients ready for the first operation list of the day.

'Come on,' Barnett said fretfully. 'Ten beds to make, and the ward to get cleaned in the next half-hour – come *on*.'

Bridget had no more time to think of how she felt, for she was rushed into a whirlwind of activity by the morose Barnett. They galloped from bed to bed, pulling on blankets, beating pillows into submission, while patients either mumbled or grumbled or tried to flirt with them, depending on their age, their illness, and the moods they were in.

Bridget was a little puzzled at first at the difference between the technique of bed-making she had learned in the PTS and the rapid sketchiness of the bed-making Barnett seemed to expect of her, but she soon realised that there wasn't any time for the leisurely perfectionism of the classroom, and she followed Barnett's quick movements with gradually increasing speed of her own.

And then, there were lockers to polish, bed-tables to wash, empty water-jugs to be collected, washed, and refilled, and Bridget scuttled after Barnett through these jobs like a giddy little squirrel. It seemed impossible to Bridget that the untidiness and general bustle would ever settle before Sister arrived on the ward at eight o'clock, half an hour after the rest of the staff, but somehow, every job seemed to get done at once. When Sister arrived, cool and crisp in her blue uniform, the patients were all in bed, the maid was busily pushing each bed back against the wall, having finished her sweeping, a senior nurse was checking the injections to be given to the patients waiting, red-blanketed, white-capped, and meek, on their trolleys to go to theatre for their operations, and Barnett and Bridget were bringing the last of the flowers in from the kitchen, where the staff nurse had been rearranging them.

The other day nurses finished tidying the beds, made sure the last locker was in position, and all of them, day and night nurses, came to cluster round Sister at her desk to hear the day's duties, and an account of the previous night's activities. As she stood in line with the others, at the very end as behoved her lowly position as junior pro, Bridget carefully put her hands behind her, as the others had, painfully aware of the smudge of dirt on her apron, put there by a dirty ashtray she had removed all too hastily from a particularly cluttered locker, and feeling her cap wobbling insecurely on her head.

Sister let her eye run along the line of nurses, stopping at Barnett and Bridget.

'I realise that as juniors, you two have rather dirty jobs to do – but that doesn't mean you can go about my ward looking like ragamuffins,' she said severely. 'If you can't keep cleaner than that, you'd better wear plastic aprons when you do your cleaning. How do you suppose patients feel having to look at people as messy as you two?' She looked at Bridget then. 'Now – you're fresh from PTS, so we mustn't be too hard on you, must we? But remember, this is a clean ward, and my nurses must be clean – ' She peered closer at Bridget then. 'Heaven help us, aren't you the clumsy one who used hot milk to wash the floor when you came here?'

Bridget blushed scarlet, and mumbled, 'Yes, Sister. Sorry, Sister.' And Sister threw her eyes up in mock horror and said to the other nurses, 'Keep an eye on this one, Nurses – she'll need training not to break and spill everything in sight.' Which was hardly fair, Bridget thought miserably. Anyone can have one accident, for heaven's sake –

The other nurses giggled obediently, clearly seeing that Sister expected them to, and one of the senior nurses winked companionably at Bridget, which made her feel better, while the morose Barnett sniffed at her side.

Sister then plunged into her reading of the night report, and Bridget listened carefully, trying to make some sense out of what she heard. The man in bed one was well, he'd slept well, and his colostomy had worked well – what was a colostomy? wondered Bridget – and pushed the word to the back of her mind as Sister went on inexorably. Bed two, Herniorrhaphy for today's list, slept well last night, ready prepped this morning. Bed three second on the list for a lumbar sympathectomy, needed sedatives in the night, very nervous man – and so it went on, till Bridget's head reeled with patients' names, with unfamiliar diseases, odd abbreviations – what was Mag. Tri. Co., for pity's sake? – feeling hopelessly that she would never in a million years learn enough to understand what it was all about. The things she had learned in PTS – about the structure and function of the heart, for example, and about the workings of a sewage farm – had no apparent relevance to any of the things she had heard this morning.

But before she could think about this further, Sister was reading out the day's off-duty rota. 'Let me know what days off you want by tomorrow at the latest, please, Nurses, and I'll do my best to oblige – ' She smiled up at Bridget then, her really rather pretty face smooth and young in the morning sunshine. 'You'll

find me very good about off-duty, Nurse Preston – '
The others nodded in eager agreement. 'If you want
any particular off-duty for a special date, or a party
or whatever, let me know, and I'll do my best to help
– but I expect you to be willing and cheerful about
changes if I have to make them in an emergency. Fair
enough?' And Bridget, confused and blushing again,
nodded speechlessly.

'For the rest,' Sister went on, 'all I ask of you on my
ward is willingness to learn, *constant* thoughtfulness for
the patients, and a modicum of commonsense. If there's
something you don't understand, come and ask me – for
God's sake don't take chances on doing things if you are
in any doubt. Nurse Barnett there, now. Last week she
gave a man a drink of water ten minutes before he was
due in theatre – the whole list had to be rearranged. So
remember, if you're in any doubt, *ask*. And don't mind
even if I'm angry at the time. I may bark, but I've never
been known to bite, right, Nurses?'

'Right,' the others chorused, even the sulky Barnett,
and then scattered about the morning's work, some
to be off duty till lunch-time, others to finish getting
the ward ready for the morning's operation lists, and
consultants' and registrars' rounds. Bridget was sent to
tidy herself, change her apron, and drink her morning
coffee, and to come back immediately after that. Her
off-duty time was to be that afternoon.

When she came back to the ward, half an hour
later, it was quiet, the men reading papers or dozing
in their white-counterpaned beds, the long, polished
floor gleaming in patches as sunshine poured in through
the tall windows and lit the long room to a bright
butter-yellow. She stood for a moment, looking down
the ward, and suddenly she liked what she saw, for-
getting her nervousness. It was quiet, a nurse moving
softly along the beds, distributing morning medicines,
another at the far end taking 10 a.m. temperatures,

while a clatter of dishes came from the kitchen where Kitty the wardmaid was washing up. It all looked and sounded so peaceful, so safe, like an oversized nursery full of oversized babies.

And then sister came up behind her – Nanny? thought Bridget wryly, still with her nursery simile – then banished the thought as sister said crisply, 'Now, Nurse Preston, I'm going to start the morning's dressing round, and you are going to come with me. I will do the dressings, and you will help me, and *learn*. Listen to what I say, store the things I will tell you in a tidy corner of your mind, and you will be glad of it when your final exams come round. We'll set the trolleys now, and then start.'

Together, Sister and Bridget put masks over their mouths and noses – Sister lecturing Bridget severely on the technique of using masks meanwhile – and Bridget stood in awe and admiration as Sister deftly removed steaming bowls and instruments from the huge steriliser in the sterilising room at the end of the ward, using long forceps, moving the things about on the trolleys with the ease of long practice.

And then they began. From bed to bed, removing stitches, shortening drainage tubes, cleaning infected incisions – the tasks were many, often extremely unpleasant, sometimes decidedly smelly. Bridget was sent scuttling from bedside to sterilising room, clearing used trolleys, emptying receivers of their dirty dressings with averted eyes – they really were so very unpleasant, some of them, particularly the colostomy one. Bridget told herself with heartfelt certainty that she would never again have to ask what a colostomy was. And then Sister would arrive like a young tornado behind her chivvying her to hurry, sending clouds of steam bellying through the room as she laid her next trolley, shooing the now almost exhausted Bridget in front of her.

The dressings began to get nastier and dirtier. As

Sister explained, surgically clean dressings were done first – others, the kind that showed infection quickly, like prostatectomy incisions, were done later. As she stood beside the beds, Bridget began to feel decidedly queasy. Some of the wounds they were dressing really did look very nasty, some of the smells – of the lotions on the trolleys as much as those of the dressings – so unfamiliar and pungent that her head swam and she wished with all her being that she had been able to eat something at breakfast that morning. Somehow, she told herself hazily, it would have been better if I didn't feel so horribly empty.

It was while they were doing a complicated dressing that involved Bridget having to hold a pair of forceps to keep part of the original dressing out of the way while Sister clipped stitches and shortened the red rubber drainage tube in the wound, that the screen behind Bridget parted. She could not look round, even had she wanted to. It was taking all her will power to keep her swimming head up, to keep her shaking hands holding the forceps, to just keep on her feet, so wobbly and sick was she feeling now.

'Morning, Sister! How's my favourite Sister this morning?' said a cheerful voice. 'As beautiful as ever?'

Sister bridled and her eyes crinkled above her mask as she smiled, and the patient grinned too, relieved at the interruption. He wasn't really enjoying her ministrations very much.

'Good morning, Mr Simpson,' he said, equally cheerfully, as Josh came round from behind Bridget, still bending over her forceps. He peered interestedly at her, above her mask, for Josh was a man who looked at every girl he ever came across as a matter of course, and the clefts in his cheeks deepened suddenly as he grinned at her.

'Well, blow me, if it isn't the Tiddler!' he said. 'First day in the slaughterhouse, is it?' and he winked at the patient, who winked back, and laughed hoarsely. This was his fifth operation in two years, and he had been in and out of this ward so often that he felt a proprietary interest in the lives of all the people who worked in it.

'Ain't she a quiet little mouse, Mr Simpson?' the patient said, grinning at Bridget. 'Never said a word yet, she 'asn't.'

Bridget felt rather than saw Sister's displeasure, and the faint frown that appeared between her smooth eyebrows. But Bridget was feeling much too ill to care now, her head whirling as the people and things around her seemed to swirl and dip in sickening waves.

And then, another nurse put her head round the screens, and said urgently to Sister, 'Matron's on the 'phone, Sister – wants to speak to you at once – '

And Sister, muttering slightly at the interruption, said, 'I'll have to go – Nurse Preston, just hold those forceps like that, and I'll be right back – sorry, Mr Simpson – and you, Mr Jeffcoate, mind you keep your inquisitive fingers away from that dressing while I'm gone – ' and she slid away between the screen to go purposefully up the ward to the telephone. Josh perched himself on the side of the bed, and with a wink at Mr Jeffcoate, said to Bridget, 'Well, Tiddler? How goes it? Do you think you'll last the next three years?'

But his voice came to Bridget from miles away, seeming to echo in her ears, as waves of blackness and speckles seemed to wash over her. She just heard Mr Jeffcoate say indignantly, ''ere, watch out will yer – ' before she passed clean out.

She came round almost immediately, to find Josh holding on to her, gently pulling her away from the bedside, while the indignant Mr Jeffcoate held protective hands across his abdomen. He had only just prevented Bridget from falling heavily on to it, and was still shaking with reaction from the fright she had given him.

'Silly Tiddler – why didn't you say you'd come over all queer like? It happens to all of us some time or another – didn't eat any breakfast this morning, I'll bet you.'

Bridget leaned against him gratefully, feeling his broad shoulders behind her, his hands on her arms, holding her firm, and managed a watery smile. 'No – ' she murmured. 'I didn't, I am afraid – and then all the dressings – '

He nodded sympathetically, but she could feel the laughter bubbling in him. 'I do wish you could have seen Mr Jeffcoate's face,' he said, still holding her firm. 'Thought you were going to squash him flat, he did, didn't you, Mr J?' and the patient, now reassured he was safe from any such accident, grinned back.

At this point, Sister reappeared behind the screens, to look at the little scene that met her eyes with a very definite frown on her face.

'What's going on here?' she asked icily. 'Nurse Preston, I told you to keep that dressing out of the way, and now look what's happened.'

'Not to worry, Sister,' Josh said soothingly. 'No harm done – and the poor little scrap couldn't help it – fainted she did! No breakfast, and then a lot of dressings – too much for a novice, especially one as tender as this.'

At the implied rebuke, Sister coloured up hotly under her mask. 'They have to learn, Mr Simpson, and the sooner the better. We can't cater to adolescent squeamishness, you know. I'm running a ward, not a girls' boarding-school, and these nurses must be trained and the patients looked after – '

'Of course, of course,' Josh said, soothingly again. 'And this girl is a silly little goose – still, I'm sure you'll make a nurse of her in time, Sister – look, I'll take her to the office, and get someone to give her a cup of hot milk and a biscuit or something, and then I'll do the round with you – all right?' and before she could answer, he pushed Bridget ahead of him and led her shaky steps down the ward towards the office and a chair.

As Kitty went scurrying off at his command to get Bridget something to eat, he plonked her down in a chair and stood looking down on her bent head.

'Poor old thing,' he said softly. 'You've had a horrible morning, haven't you?'

She nodded wordlessly, and then he squatted on his haunches in front of her and took her chin in his square, warm hand, and Bridget was aware of the faint scent of antiseptic and tobacco on it.

'Tell you what, Tiddler – I'll buy you a slap-up supper tonight to make sure you're well stoked up against tomorrow's horrors – pick you up at the home at nine – you'll be off at half past eight – and don't bother to dress up. I can only afford the local fish restaurant, anyway. OK? Take care of yourself till then – '

And with a last, friendly grin, he disappeared back into the ward, leaving Bridget mortified with shame, delighted and excited because he had asked her out, dreading facing Sister again, and wondering what on earth to do about Josh. After all, Bobby had said she'd 'seen him first' and so she had. What on earth was she to do?

Chapter 5

She got through the rest of the day somehow, dreadfully aware of Sister's displeasure, more and more aware of the fact that her feet ached with a steady, nagging insistence, worried yet happy when she remembered Josh's invitation to supper. Had she heard Sister discussing her in the Sister's dining-room that lunch-time, she would have been even more unhappy.

'I've been landed with a right little monkey,' Sister Youngs confided to the Theatre Sister, with whom she shared a table. 'One of those quiet, demure ones who looks as though butter wouldn't melt in her mouth. And do you know what she did? I turn my back for one moment, and she promptly faints in Josh Simpson's arms!'

'She shows good taste, then,' Theatre Sister drawled. 'He's one of the best-looking men we've had here for years.'

Sister Youngs sniffed. 'Precisely! If she'd fainted while I'd been there, I'd not have given it another thought – I mean, first day on the wards is a bit of a so-and-so – I know that – but the neat way she waited for someone interesting to faint on! Too smooth by half.'

Theatre Sister laughed. 'I'm damned grateful I don't get 'em fresh from PTS like you ward wallahs do. At least, by the time they're sent to theatre, the worst of the corners are rubbed off.'

'I'll rub a few corners off this one, that I will,' Sister Youngs said grimly, and put a third lump of sugar in her coffee. Sister Youngs was beginning to get decidedly fat, Theatre Sister thought smugly, and passed her a jug of cream, just to help her along. Even at Sister level there were rivalries at the Royal, and Theatre Sister and Sister Youngs had had their respective eyes on the same consultant for the past year now, and it was Sister Youngs who was making most progress with him. Hence the cream.

Bridget almost fell off duty that night. Even the three hours afternoon off-duty that she had spent in the sitting-room with her shoes off and her feet propped high on a stool, had not relieved her fatigue. Now, at half past eight, she was exhausted.

The four girls had adjacent rooms in the main Nurses' Home, and when Bridget toiled her weary way to hers, she found the others were already there, Liz and Judith sprawled on her bed, Bobby sitting at her dressing-table peering at her face in the little mirror.

'I think I am going to die, right here and now,' Judith said dramatically, lying with arms outstretched.

'Well, have the decency to do it on your own bed,' Liz said, pushing her away irritably. 'Why do you have to lie around on Bridget's bed?'

'Same reason you do,' Judith said. 'My room looks like Paddy's market – I haven't even made my bed yet.'

'You'll have Home Sister on to you like a ton of bricks, if she spots that,' Bobby said from the mirror. 'My God, just *look* at my hands! They'll be like a washerwoman's after another day like today. I've done nothing but scrub and clean and mop floors and generally act like a char – ' Then she grinned reminiscently. 'Not that Casualty doesn't have its compensations. There're some very nice men about – '

Bridget, sitting on the only remaining chair in her room, easing her shoes off, took a deep breath at this.

'Josh Simpson turned up on my ward this morning,' she said, her head down, apparently absorbed in undoing her shoes. 'Asked me out for supper tonight – coming here at nine, he said.'

There was a brief silence, then Liz said, 'Well, get our mouse! First day on the wards and she gets herself a date! I must study your technique, sweetie!'

Bridget looked up miserably at Bobby. She didn't know whether to apologise, or say she wouldn't meet Josh – though she felt that would be discourteous in the extreme, apart from her own inclinations – and was relieved and rather surprised to see that Bobby was smiling with a cat-like satisfaction.

'Well, now, there's a coincidence!' she drawled. 'David – you remember David, Bridget? – he asked *me* out to supper. Picking me up here at nine o'clock as ever is. We'll have to make up a foursome, eh, Bridie, my love?'

And Bridget smiled in relief. She had been so afraid that Bobby would be cross, would withdraw the warmth and friendship that Bridget treasured so much, also afraid she would not be able to see Josh, which she wanted to do very much indeed. And now Bobby wasn't a bit cross, and she could still see Josh. Even her feet seemed to ache less, suddenly, so happy was she.

Judith grinned across at them, and said admiringly, 'I don't know how you do it, so help me I don't. I could no more keep a date tonight than fly to the moon. Me for a hot, hot bath and blissful bed – '

'Me, too,' said Liz, and slipped off the bed to stretch and yawn hugely before padding away to her own room. 'Anyway, I've got a date with Ken for the day after tomorrow – he asked me this afternoon when I met him in the corridor on the way to dispensary – there's a lot to be said for errand running – at least you meet people and get away from those God-awful women in the ward – ' night, you lot. See you at breakfast,' and she went, followed by Judith yawning even more widely than Liz, if that were possible.

'I'll change fast,' Bobby said cheerfully, grinning at Bridget. 'Put a move on, Bridie, my love, and we'll go down together to meet the men – '

Bridget felt suddenly very shy indeed as the two of them came down the stairs twenty minutes later to see Josh and the tall, lean David leaning against the radiator waiting for them. It was Bobby, looking particularly feminine, as only she could, in tight black ski pants and a heavy red-and-yellow sweater, who ran gaily down the stairs towards them, smiling and sparkling in a way that made Bridget almost ache with envy. If only she had Bobby's gay insouciance, and her social ability, she told herself miserably, following her. Even her choice of clothes was so good, Bridget thought, painfully aware of her own sedate green skirt and matching twin set. But Josh grinned at her and said, 'You two look charming – much nicer than you do in uniform, and that's saying a lot, because you both look *very* nice in all that starch and those sexy black stockings.' And Bridget felt better, grateful to him for the ready understanding in him that was only slightly masked by his easy charm.

Almost without discussion, they went out of the building together, taking it for granted they would be a foursome. It was unfortunate for Bridget that Sister Youngs met them on the steps outside, as she came late off duty, and noticed with her sharp eye for such things that it was Josh who appeared to be squiring Bridget. The meeting only confirmed her belief that Bridget was a sly-boots who knew just how to set about getting what she wanted.

They spent an hilarious evening. Bobby and Josh were both in fine form, capping each other's jokes and sallies with ever more outrageous comments, sparkling at each other in a way that made Bridget giggle helplessly, even made the silent David smile. Bridget soon realised that David was not a man to talk much – his moroseness at the party had not been entirely due to the fact that he was drunk. He was just a man who talked little, who sat in smooth silence, observing, missing little of what went on about him. As the evening progressed, and they ate fish and chips and huge pickled onions – which Bobby and Josh both seemed to adore, even spending a noisy five minutes trying to see which of them could get the most of one particularly large onion, stuck up on a fork between them – David and Bridget became more and more like an audience, rather than participants in the evening's entertainment.

Bridget didn't mind this a bit. She was more than happy to sit in a bemused and fatigued silence, picking at her meal, watching the others – particularly Josh. She watched the way his eyes crinkled when he laughed – which was often – the way the light reflected off the fine hair on the back of his hands, the shape of the square, well-kept nails, the way his cheeks deepened into clefts when he smiled or spoke. And almost without realising it, she began to feel that this attractive man was the sort of man she liked more than any other sort. She stole a glance at the silent David, at his deep-set eyes, his narrow mouth, unsmiling and shut as tight as a trap, at the faint blue shadows under his eyes and on his temples, and thought confusedly. 'How can two men be so unlike? I wish I could be like Bobby, and talk and giggle with Josh like she does – ' But she was content just to sit and watch.

When it was time to get back to the hospital – and it was more than the curfew that decided this, for even Bobby was beginning to wilt at the end of her very long, hard day – they all walked back together. But it was Bobby who put her hand companionably into the crook of Josh's arm, and Bridget who found herself walking beside David.

And when they stood on the steps of the Home,

there was a silent, slightly embarrassed moment, until Bobby, moving very imperceptibly nearer to Josh, put her face up towards his and said softly, 'I must *reek* of pickled onions. Is it very bad – or can't you tell, because you're in the same state yourself?' And Josh, finding this very pretty face so conveniently near to his, and being a man of very friendly tendencies, accepted the clearly implied invitation, and kissed Bobby very thoroughly. And Bridget, seeing Bobby's arms go up round his neck, seeing the dark head she had come to like so much so near to Bobby's fair one, felt a stab of almost physical pain and unhappiness.

But she had no time to think about it, for to her complete surprise, David, beside her, suddenly whirled her round, held her very close, and kissed her extremely thoroughly, in a way that bruised her mouth, and made her want to pull away from him. But she couldn't move, so firm was David's grip.

When he released her at last, she pulled back, her hand against her sore mouth, and looked at him over it, her eyes shadowed in the dimness.

'Thank you for supper – er – both of you – ' She stopped, unable to look at Josh and Bobby, aware that Bobby still had her arms twined about Josh's neck, that she was holding on to him as if she had no intention of ever letting go.

'Goodnight, David,' she said again, just as David seemed about to make another lunge at her, and turned and almost ran through the door into the Home.

Josh, looking over Bobby's shoulder at the flick of green skirt disappearing, felt a sudden twinge of something rare for him – embarrassment. He had always taken his pleasures easily and gaily, not being in the least perturbed if another couple were about when he kissed a girl goodnight. After all, why should he? None of the girls he ever met had mattered to him very much, except as delightful creatures who were fun. Why care?

56

But this quiet, shy child, as he thought of her, somehow embarrassed him, making him see himself, for a fleeting moment, through someone else's eyes.

But then Bobby put up her inviting lips again, and David muttered a glum 'Goodnight' before making his way across the garden towards the courtyard and the doctor's commonroom, and Josh, left with a very pretty and willing girl, forgot his moment's embarrassment and enthusiastically co-operated with Bobby.

It was twenty minutes later when Bobby came upstairs, by which time Bridget was already in bed, lying in the darkness and staring at the dim shape of the window, trying to sort out her confused thoughts, still feeling David's experienced and alarming kiss on her mouth.

Bobby put the light on, and sat down beside Bridget, smiling at her in a warm friendliness that brought all Bridget's need for her friendship and approbation bubbling up inside her.

'Hello, love,' Bobby said softly. 'Are you at all annoyed with me?'

'Why – why should I be?' Bridget said lamely.

'Well, it was *you* that Josh asked out – and we did change partners, didn't we?'

'He – he only asked me out of pity – because I fainted,' Bridget said honestly. 'I mean – I'm not his type, am I? He – he needs someone like you, who can talk like he does – '

Bobby, with a sort of rueful smile on her face, said, 'Well, I think you could be right, lovey – '

'And you did see him first, anyway – ' Bridget was trying not to remember the sharp pain she had felt when she saw Bobby kissing Josh, trying to forget the way Josh had looked in the restaurant, the way his eyes looked when he smiled, the warm notes of his voice, the way his hands had felt on her shoulders that morning,

57

when he had caught her and stopped her from fainting all over Mr Jeffcoate.

'Oh, please – ' Bobby seemed suddenly embarrassed. 'I know I said that at the party, but I'd had a drink or two, you know, and – well – I mean, if I thought Josh liked you best, I wouldn't *dream* of trying anything with him. I mean, a girl's got her pride, hasn't she? But it just seems to me that really David likes you better than he likes me – he *did* kiss you goodnight.'

'That was just because I was there,' Bridget said, with a surprising shrewdness. 'I think he's the sort who doesn't really notice people – I mean, a girl is a girl – not a *person*.'

'Nonsense!' Bobby scoffed. 'Of course he likes you best – and I rather think that Josh likes *me* – which is tidy and convenient, to say the least!' She smiled with sudden reminiscence. 'He certainly *behaved* as if he liked me, downstairs just now – ' and Bridget dropped her gaze, feeling the sharp pain of acute – what? She didn't know, but she certainly felt it. Maybe it was shame, she thought miserably, because it *is* shaming when a man asks you out from pity, and then prefers someone else's company. 'I'm so tired I could sleep for a week – I'm for bed, sweetie. And Josh says there'll be another party in the mess next week, and of course we're all invited – Liz'll be tickled to death. She's mad about that Ken of hers – ' Night, Bridget. See you at breakfast.'

' 'Night,' Bridget echoed, and then lay in the dark for a long time, staring at the window, trying to sleep, but too mixed up and almost too tired to.

She woke next morning feeling heavy-headed and leaden-limbed, dragging herself on duty to face another day of hard work, of Barnett's nagging, who as next in seniority was Bridget's guide about the ward, to face Sister's now definite dislike of her, to the sounds and sights and smells of the ward that seemed so dreadful to her.

But she survived the day, the long hours of running about the ward, the bed-pan and bottle rounds, the sluice scrubbing, the fetching and carrying, the bed-making and locker polishing, the serving and collection of meals, the washing of patients – everything. And she survived the next day and the next, till suddenly she realised that it wasn't quite as hard work as it had been, that the patients were no longer an amorphous crowd of frightening people, but individuals, some nice, some unpleasant, some cheerful, some perpetually moaning.

She began to like the work she did, to take a real pleasure in the muttered 'Thank you' from a man whose bed she had made more comfortable, to enjoy the appreciation with which a very ill patient sipped the orange juice she had prepared for him, to appreciate the way a man would be grateful for a friendly word from her while she cleaned his locker. Even the really difficult jobs, like helping a grown man with a bedpan, a man so miserably embarrassed by her ministrations that he almost wept with it, became worth doing. She learned, gradually, how to help the men lose their shame, learned how to be relaxed and make *them* relaxed.

She became quicker in her work about the ward, more deft, and managed to avoid the clumsiness that so enraged Sister Youngs, so that that lady began to develop a grudging respect for Bridget, began to wonder if she had misjudged her.

'Certainly,' she told Sister Chessman, at the end of Bridget's first month on the ward. 'She learns fast. And she seems to care about the patients as people, which is important. I know they like her, which is a good sign. I mean, if she was just putting on a show for me, when I was around, the men'd soon see through it, and let me know they didn't like her – Apart, as I say, from a possible tendency to be a bit of an exhibitionist when it suits her, I think she'll make a fairly good nurse – ' And Sister Chessman marked Bridget's file with a query, and sighed, wondering whether she too, had been misjudging Bridget. This was, after all, a good ward report, compared with some she had received on others in the new class.

Rather to Bridget's relief, the projected party in the mess had to be cancelled, because of a sudden epidemic of flu among the medical staff – so many men were off sick there was no time for a party, even if any of them had wanted to have one without their missing colleagues. For the same reason Bridget saw little of a very busy Josh, only sometimes scuttling past him on ward rounds, while she ran one of the lowly errands that were her lot, blushing when he managed a friendly wink in her direction.

And then, one morning in early May, when there was at last a real hint of summer in the air, Bridget was in the little cupboard that ran off the lobby of the ward – the cupboard used for testing urine specimens – scrubbing the shelves and relabelling the bottles. She was singing under her breath, quite enjoying the job, taking an almost housewifely pleasure in the tidy shelves, the freshly scrubbed wooden working surface, the gleam of the chrome taps over the tiny sink.

Josh put his head round the door and grinned at the flushed face that met his eyes, the roughened hands that were busily rubbing at a recalcitrant spot on the wooden shelf above her.

'Hello, Tiddler. Thought I heard your mellifluous tones as I hurried by on my errands of mercy – going to give the push to at least three of your patients this morning, I am – how's things in your little world?'

She felt her heart lurch sickeningly inside her at the nearness of him, the smile in his eyes so close to hers, and swallowed.

'Er – er, hello,' she said awkwardly, avoiding his eyes,

60

and scrubbing busily at the now vanished spot. 'Fine, thanks. How are you?'

'Worked to death as usual,' he said, leaning against the door, and smiling down at her obvious confusion. 'Honestly, Tiddler, you are sweet. I've never met anyone as shy as you are – really I haven't.'

She didn't answer, wishing desperately that she could, but completely unable to think of the sort of flippant, gay thing Bobby would have said in the same situation.

'You know, Tiddler.' He was almost serious suddenly. 'I never did apologise for what happened that night we all went out to supper.'

'Apologise? What for?' Bridget was genuinely surprised. It had never occurred to her that Josh had anything to apologise for. Admittedly, he had taken her out, and should, in all courtesy, have spent the evening concentrating on her, but if she herself was too dull to interest him it was hardly any fault of Josh's – or so she argued within herself.

'Well, never mind,' he said, a little shy himself for once, and then smiled again. 'Listen, let me make it up to you – what say we go out for a drive somewhere tomorrow? Hmm? Spring is really and truly here at last, and we could get out to the country in no time in my old jalopy – poor but hard working, like me, that car. What do you say?'

She looked at him then, part of her aching to say, 'Yes – oh, yes please!' and his eyes looked down at her in a way that made her head swim suddenly, delightfully. But almost without thinking about it, she heard Bobby's voice in her mind's ear, 'I mean, a girl's got her pride, hasn't she? – if I thought Josh liked you best, I wouldn't dream of trying anything with him – he certainly behaved as if he liked me – '

And even though I'm dull, Bridget thought desperately, looking up at the face above hers, a face she was

61

coming to care a great deal for, even if I am dull and a bit stupid about men, I've got my pride too. He only asked me out of pity the first time – and now he's asking me out of pity again, because he really likes Bobby better than me, and thinks I might be hurt –

'No – no thank you,' she said baldly, and dropped her gaze before the look of surprise on his face, dropped her eyes too soon to see that he was hurt as well as surprised.

'Phew – !' he said after a moment, his voice a little strained. 'Well, that's me told off! I didn't mean to make you as mad as that, you know. No need to bite my head off – '

She could have wept at that. If he'd only understand how hard she found it to talk to men, how little experience she had of saying 'no' gracefully –

'I didn't mean to be rude – ' she managed. 'It's just that – well, I'm rather busy just now – '

'Oh, well, not to worry!' he said, with an apparent return of his usual cheerfulness. 'Sorry I bothered you – see you!' and he was gone, on into the ward to drink coffee with a friendly Sister Youngs, and go through the notes of the patients to be discharged. And Bridget was left in her little cupboard, still scrubbing shelves, but with every scrap of sunshine gone out of her day. But a girl's got her pride, she told herself stubbornly. And I can't bear to be pitied. So that's that.

Chapter 6

Spring made its reluctant change to summer, and suddenly, their first three months as full students at the Royal were past, and Bridget and her class found themselves in the heady position of having a class junior to them in the hospital. They moved from the Lambing Pen, in the dining room, behind the door, to the next table up, where they ate their meals in gay and relaxed postures, so that the new juniors at the table behind the door could steal admiring and awed glances at them, just as they had themselves in the days when they had been fresh out of PTS.

The new class meant, too, that a reshuffle of staff was necessary, and Bridget found herself assigned to the Casualty department. Bobby was sent to the Male Surgical ward, a move which delighted her, Judith to the Out-patient department, and Liz to one of the Children's wards, which pleased her rather – she had a genuine liking for children, and found that most of them liked her, which was half the battle in any form of child care.

In one way, Bridget was relieved to be away from Male Surgical. It meant she would see less of Josh, who, as senior surgical registrar, inevitably spent a lot of time there. Ever since that day when Bridget had so baldly refused to go out with him, he had seemed to Bridget to change somehow. He was still friendly, still gay, and amusing when he met her, but in an oddly distant way. He didn't call her Tiddler, for example, a nickname she had liked to hear on his lips, made no further attempt to talk to her on her own. And this helped a bit – but not much. For Bridget couldn't deny to herself that Josh had become a very important person in her life, yet she knew she had no right to regard him as anything other than an acquaintance. Every time she saw him, she felt her knees shake, something deep inside her taking a sickening lurch, felt her face flame with a hot blush. But even as she felt so, she reminded herself sternly that he was Bobby's friend, not hers. It was Bobby he took out, Bobby he kissed 'Goodnight' on the Home doorstep, Bobby who always sat next to him when they went out in a crowd, as they often did.

This was the hardest part of it all, she would tell herself bleakly. They often went out in a noisy group of eight, the four girls, with Josh escorting Bobby, Ken escorting Liz, and a fresh-faced young anaesthetist called Clive Damant escorting Judith, and the silent David always with Bridget. It was odd, really, she would tell herself, undressing wearily after these evenings out. David has never once asked me out in so many words – he's hardly said more than a few words to me, anyway. Yet we seem to be stuck with each other.

And indeed, so it was. Bobby, still the prime mover in the tight little group, would come bouncing into her room, to tell her cheerfully that they were all going out to a cinema, or on a country pub crawl, or to eat hot-dogs and hamburgers at the funfair in Battersea, or whatever she and Josh had planned between them. Neither Liz nor Judith had the least objection to having plans like this made for them, as long as they were assured that Clive and Ken would be there, and when Bridget once said to Bobby that she didn't want to go, Bobby had flown into a furious temper.

'But I just don't want to go out tonight – I'm tired – we've been terribly busy on Cas, and I want to go to bed early – ' Bridget said pleadingly.

But Bobby wouldn't hear of it. They were all friends weren't they? she asked in a voice that made the tired Bridget shiver suddenly.

'And if we are, it means we do things in a crowd – we like to be together. If you want to turn into a drear like that Jackson, or a swot or something, just say the word, and we'll keep out of your way. If you don't want us, we don't want you – '

And inevitably, Bridget went out with the crowd, to sit again with David, to listen to the others chatter, to try not to watch the way Bobby snuggled close to Josh at every possible opportunity, to try not to see the way he would drop casual kisses on her upturned face, or would sit with an arm round her waist.

Even the way David took it for granted that she, too, wanted to neck, like the others, was something she learned to tolerate. She couldn't pretend, even to herself, that she really liked his kisses, or even accorded him more than the casual regard she had for any of the others – except Josh of course. But she couldn't bear the thought of being shut out of the company of her three friends. Even though she had been at the Royal for more than six months now, she had made no other friends. The four of them were so self-contained, there had been no real opportunity for her to make friends among any of the other nurses. They had formed their own groups and cliques and there was no room for Bridget in any of them. If she had not had Bobby and Liz and Judith, she would have been quite without friends, and the thought of returning to the loneliness of her previous existence made her shudder.

But in spite of the ever-present ache about Josh, in spite of the depressing tedium of having David kiss and fondle her, she was happy. Casualty was an exciting and interesting place in which to work, and as she became more senior, she was taught to do ever more complicated work in the department. She learned to apply dressings, to bandage wounds and help put plaster casts on broken limbs, to give injections, to assist in the minor operating room attached to the department, and she gloried in her new skills, and took a real pride and interest in her work. Casualty Sister seemed to like her, which was refreshing to say the least, after the sort of armed truce her relationship with Sister Youngs in Male Surgical had been.

She found time, too, to study, to keep up with the lectures that they attended during the week, to plan her work for the next study block the class would go to, just before their Preliminary State Examinations. She would spend hours of her daytime off duty in the classroom, reading and studying for the sheer pleasure of it, enjoying tracking down information about a patient she may have seen in the course of her work in Casualty; but she never told the others about the time she spent thus, knowing quite well that they would laugh at her, sneer almost, for all three of the others had short patience for the people they scornfully labelled as swots.

And then, late one evening, just before she was due off duty, she was in the department rolling bandages ready for the next morning's dressing clinic, alone with one of the very few juniors from the class after hers, while Sister was off duty for the evening, and the staff nurse in charge had slipped off to have a quiet natter with a friend on one of the wards. The department was completely empty of patients, and the staff nurse, a rather giddy girl with a decidedly underdeveloped sense of responsibility, told Bridget that if anything came in, she was to cope if she could, and if she couldn't, to send the junior to find her.

Bridget was enjoying herself. The department was so clean and quiet, the junior singing unmelodiously in the sluice as she washed that day's dirty bandages, and Bridget was at peace. The late sunshine of a summer evening slanted across the tiled floor, lighting the flowered cubicle curtains to an incongruous gaiety, glancing off the chrome and enamel of the instrument cupboards, while the sterilisers hissed contentedly in the corner, and the distant sounds of people in the courtyard outside came through the big double doors. Bridget was to have a day off next day, and as none of the others had days off to coincide, she had planned to spend it all alone, sight-seeing around London, for as a Northerner there was still a delight for her in behaving like a tourist in London.

She had just tucked the last bandage into its box, and was stretching in luxurious relaxation, when the rough, urgent peal of an ambulance bell cut across the peace of the big department. Bridget felt her heart fall with a sickening thump; an emergency – and Staff Nurse wasn't here and would be furious if Bridget sent for her before finding out just what the case was. Perhaps it's for the Maternity department, she told herself with hope, even as she hurried across the big floor to open the curtains of one of the cubicles, to get it ready for a possible case. Her hope was short-lived, for the big double doors swished open and two ambulance men almost tumbled through, pushing a trolley as fast as they could.

'Bleeding – ' one of them muttered, as he manoeuvred the trolley towards the opened cubicle. 'And he's damn' near 'ad it, I reckon – where do you want 'im, Nurse? – '

Bridget stared down at the patient on the trolley, almost paralysed with fear, all her new-found skills and knowledge seeming to melt away. 'What do I do now?' she asked herself in desperation. 'What do I do now – '

There was a youth on the trolley, a fair boy, with straight hair flopping into half closed eyes, with faint rims of blue showing under the lax eyelids. He was waxen white, his skin showing the faint blue-green tinge of extreme blood loss. One arm was clumsily wrapped in a big bath towel, and the gaudy reds and blues of the pattern on the towel seemed smudged with the much brighter red that was spreading over it with ominous rapidity.

'Put him on the couch,' Bridget managed. 'I'll help you – '

Behind her, she heard the double doors swish open again, and she looked up, praying it was Staff Nurse come back, but it was a woman, a woman with the same sort of fair hair as the boy on the trolley, a face twisted with fear, and streaked with tears, yet obviously enough like that of the patient to make it clear she was a relative.

'If you'll just wait in the waiting room,' Bridget said, with the automatic brightness she had learned to use when dealing with anxious relatives, 'I'll call the doctor, and he'll see you as soon as he's examined the patient – '

'Hurry 'im, then – please, get the doctor quick – he's a bleeder, see, he's a bleeder – it won't stop, no matter what, it won't stop – told 'im I did, been telling 'im all 'is life – you're a bleeder, I told him, don't go playing with things what might start you off, but 'e won't listen, you know what boys is, and 'e wouldn't listen – make the doctor 'urry, Nurse, get 'im quick – e's a bleeder, see, like my dad – a bleeder – '

Bridget stared at her in bewilderment while the ambulance men fussed over the boy on the trolley, lifting him onto the couch.

'A bleeder?' she said stupidly. 'A bleeder – like your dad?'

'That's right – ' The woman came close, and putting her hands on Bridget's arms, shook her in urgency. ''e's a *bleeder* – 'e needs some of that snake stuff – do 'urry – for Christ's sake, *'urry.*'

68

And then, something she had read in one of her long mornings in the classroom came back into her head, and almost without thinking Bridget called quickly to the nervous junior who was standing hovering on the outskirts of the little group.

'Get the surgeon on duty, Nurse Stead – and then call Staff Nurse – as fast as you can – ' and as the junior scuttled for the phone, Bridget ran across the big room towards the tall medicine cupboard on the far side.

'Please God, let there be some. Please God, let there be some,' she prayed urgently under her breath, as she scrabbled through shelves, not completely sure what she was looking for, but hoping she would know it when she saw it. She could feel the stillness behind her, the urgency in the ambulance men and the fair woman, all standing helplessly watching her, and she let her eyes run across the shelves, looking desperately for something she prayed she would recognise when she saw it.

And then, tucked at the back of a shelf, she did see it. A small box with a dimly written label. 'Russell's Viper Venom. Packed in Fibrin gauze. Sterile.'

With hands shaking with a mixture of fear and relief, she grabbed the box, and almost slid across the floor in her hurry. The ambulance men without a word stepped back, one of them leading the frightened woman away towards the waiting room while the other stationed himself behind the couch, ready to help Bridget.

With infinitely careful fingers, her heart seeming to be in her mouth, she began to unwrap the now completely bloodsodden towel. As the last fold came away from the arm, she could see the really comparatively small cut that was causing the trouble, a mere inch long, but from which blood was pouring, an ominous bright red, completely unclotted, liquid. The towel that had been wrapped round it showed no sign of a clot

69

anywhere, unlike most blood-soaked things Bridget had seen before.

With her lower lip clenched between her teeth, she mopped at the cut with a big swab from the little table ready set up beside the couch, as in all the cubicles, and with a sign to the ambulance man, let him hold the swab firmly over the cut while she opened the precious box she had found in the cupboard. The pads of sponge-like yellow fibrin gauze tumbled out into the dressing-bowl on the trolley, and with a pair of forceps, she picked up one piece after another – there were three – and pressed them onto the wound, dropping the already soaked swab onto the trolley beside her. Then, she piled thick pads of cotton wool on top, and strapped them down with sticky tape the sensible ambulance man had cut ready for her as she worked. And then they both stood there, staring down at the dressing, not much whiter than the skin of the arm against which it lay.

Bridget stood, absurdly aware of the sounds from the courtyard outside, the clatter of wheels and drums as the sterilising porter went by with his load of drums to be baked in the big autoclaves of the main operating theatres, the high voices of children passing by in the street outside, on the other side of the department. As she stared at the makeshift dressing she had put on, her eyes never shifting from it.

A patch of blood appeared in the centre, spread slowly. She found herself praying, confusedly – 'Please let it work – please let Staff Nurse come back soon – please let it work – '

Then, after a long pause, she let out the breath she had been unconsciously holding.

'What do you think?' she asked the ambulance man, still standing silently beside the couch. 'What do you think?'

'I think you've done it, Nurse – that patch hasn't changed last minute or so, has it?'

'I thought it hadn't – ' she murmured, and stood staring still. But the patch didn't grow any bigger, just remaining in the middle of the snowy cotton wool dressing as an uneven splodge of vivid red. Maybe she *had* done it – ?

The doors swished, and footsteps clattered purposefully across the terrazzo tiles, and the cubicle curtains billowed as Josh appeared at the side of the couch.

'What gives?' he asked gaily. 'Some hysterical child on the phone rang the common room with some garbled tale about a blood bath down here – I'm not on Casualty call, but I thought I'd better come – oh, hello, there!' and he grinned in a friendly way as he recognised Bridget standing still, leaning over the silent pale boy on the couch.

'Bleeder, sir,' said the ambulance man with cheerful officiousness. 'Got a call from the other side of the railway station there – found this feller goin' like a stuck pig – 'is mum said 'e'd been muckin' around with a hammer and chisel – anyway, he was damn near right out then, and by the time we got 'im 'ere, 'e was right out – and bleeding! – cor, never saw so much blood in all my natural, and I've seen a bit in my time, I can tell yer!' He grinned with a sort of horrible relish – 'Bleeding like a stuck pig, 'e was – you should just see our ambulance – '

'Mmm – ' Josh pushed him to one side with an inoffensive gesture, and the ambulance man gave way, leaving Josh to bend over the boy, one hand on his pulse, the other lifting one eyelid with a practised gesture.

'My God, but he's exanguinated – ' he muttered.

Bridget lifted her eyes for the first time from her dressing, in which the tell-tale splodge of blood had made no change, smiled shakily at Josh, and said, 'He must be – that towel was wrapped round him – ' and she indicated the sopping wet towel on the floor at the foot of the couch.

71

Josh looked at it, and nodded crisply. 'What did you do?' he asked, as he touched her dressing on the lax arm with delicate fingers.

'I – I hope it was right,' she said, suddenly remembering just how junior she was, frightened in case she had done the wrong thing. 'His mother said her father was the same, and I thought – I read it somewhere – I put Russell's Viper Venom on it – '

'You were absolutely right – '. He smiled at her warmly. 'I've seen this boy before – he's a haemophiliac all right. If you hadn't put the venom on he'd have been dead by now – as it is, he's in a pretty bad state – well done, Tiddler – '

And then, Staff Nurse came clacking across the department, summoned from her cosy chat on the ward by the frightened junior, her face a picture of guilt.

'Sorry, Mr Simpson,' she said, lying bravely. 'I had to go away for a moment – '

'Not to worry, Staff,' Josh said, grinning at her obvious confusion. 'Your deputy here did nobly and well. A proper little life-saver, eh?' and Bridget felt the all too ready blush climb into her cheeks.

'Better get this boy to a ward,' Josh said. 'And we'll need some blood for him – chase up his notes, Staff, will you? There's a record in them about his blood group, and I'll take some from that sopping towel for a cross match – jump about now!'

And in record time, the boy was whisked away to a medical ward, while a medical registrar came and relieved Josh of his cross-matching job. By the time the night staff arrived, and Bridget was free to go shakily off duty, feeling desperately tired as a sort of reaction to the fright of the past half-hour, Josh too was free to go.

He hurried across the courtyard after her, and caught her up at the gate to the Nurses' garden.

'You did very well, Tiddler,' he said, his voice warm. 'You showed a presence of mind not many as young and inexperienced as you could have managed. Well done.'

'Thank you,' she murmured, agonisingly aware of his warm hand on her arm. 'I – I'm glad I remembered – '

'He'll be glad too, I imagine,' he said dryly. Then, with a pressure of his hand, he held her back, as she started to try to go on through the gate. 'Listen, Tiddler – isn't it time you and I got to know each other a little better? When we're with the crowd, I never get the chance to talk to you – '

She bit her lip. 'I – I'm sorry – ' she said awkwardly.

He smiled then. 'You're always apologising,' he said, and his voice was teasing. 'Nothing to apologise for. What say you and I take an evening out on our own, hmm?'

She looked up at him miserably, at the handsome square face, the friendly eyes looking at her so warmly, and let her own gaze slide away.

'I can't,' she said. 'There's Bobby – and David.' Why she said David's name she wasn't quite sure. Somehow, she felt obscurely ashamed. Josh knew, knew perfectly well, that she and David had spent time necking, that he had kissed her and fondled her, just as Josh himself had behaved the same way with Bobby, and she wanted to explain how little she cared for David, feeling that quite apart from Bobby's claim on Josh, she could not possibly go out with Josh if he thought she cared for David at all. But he misunderstood – and why shouldn't he? she thought miserably – I'm so bad at explaining.

Misunderstand he certainly did, for his hand dropped from her arm and his face closed suddenly.

'Yes – yes, of course – ' he said. 'Sorry to be so silly – I'll see you around, then,' and he turned and went, striding across the now dusky courtyard back towards the lights of the main hospital. And Bridget stood at the gate on the edge of tears, feeling a mixture of reaction

73

to the episode in Casualty, kicking herself mentally because of the way she always said the wrong thing to this man, a man she cared far too much about for her own peace of mind.

Chapter 7

The last brown leaves from the trees carpeted the courtyard with dangerous wet drifts, and the November wind sent them swirling messily in all directions, as the four girls hurried across on their way to the main hospital. Bridget felt her knees shake as she thought of the interview to come, though the other three chattered cheerfully enough. She could not tell them how scared she was or even why, since they seemed so unconcerned. And why should I be scared? she asked herself with an attempted reasonableness. Everyone has to see Matron to get their second-year belts – but it made no difference. She was scared.

The four weeks of the Preliminary State Block were behind them, the examinations had been written, the vivas struggled through, and now the results were out. Bridget hadn't found the exams too difficult, the long hours of study she had spent standing her in good stead. And the other three, needing constant help as usual, had badgered her to hear their learning, to check their notes for them, and this had helped Bridget's own studies, too. It was odd, somehow, how quickly the past year had gone, yet how slowly too. It seemed to her she had spent her whole life at the Royal, that she had known no other existence. It had been a happy year, most of it, except for the ever constant ache about Josh. For the status quo was maintained. The four girls and their regular escorts still went about together, their relationships with the men seeming to change little, though it was obvious that Liz and Ken were very deeply in love with each other – certainly more genuinely attached than any of the others were.

Bobby still went about with Josh most of the time, though Bridget knew she also went out with other men on the staff, and, while on holiday, with men from her home town in Surrey. Bobby was rarely in her room during her free time – always out with someone, and in a way Bridget was glad she had so many boy-friends. It made her dates with Josh less hurtful somehow. Maybe one day Bobby will tire of Josh? she would think sometimes, and then push the thought away. Even if she did, it would make no difference. Since that evening in Casualty he had never again made any attempt to ask Bridget out on her own, made no sign that he regarded her as any more than just one of the crowd.

David was a problem, though. Still morose, still not particularly communicative about himself, still he seemed perfectly happy to escort Bridget on all the group outings, still took it for granted that they would make casual love at the end of the evening. She had come to loathe those silent hours spent in the front of his car, or in the Nurses' garden, sitting on a bench under a tree. She often tried to tell him she didn't really like necking with him, didn't want to go out with him. But she could never find words, and anyway, he would take no notice, stopping her from speaking by seizing her and kissing her. There had been a couple of occasions when he had tried extremely hard to go a great deal farther than just kissing, moving his hands over her body in a way that made her go rigid with fear, once even made her pull roughly away from him and run stumbling across the garden to the safety of the Nurses' Home.

She had hoped, after that evening, that he would at last realise how she felt, and make no further attempts, but he behaved as though it had never happened. And when Bridget tried to tell Bobby that she didn't really like David, that she didn't want to go out with him any more, even if it meant not going out with the group at all – which would have been the best solution for Bridget, meaning she would not need to see Josh with Bobby – Bobby had become very angry. It was odd, she thought sometimes. I need Bobby and Liz and Judith, and I know I need them. Life without them would be dreadful. But why does Bobby need me? She must, or she wouldn't get so angry when I try to opt out of going out. I suppose she *must* need me and the others, though I can't think why. She could make friends with anyone, she's so gay, and so much fun –

No doubt about it, the happiness of the past year had nothing to do with Bridget's private life. It was in the time she spent working that she found pleasure, a deep, very real pleasure that almost surprised her. She found a sort of love, compounded of pity and, of practical sympathy welling up in her when she was with patients, an enormous satisfaction in being able to make ill people comfortable, do something real and constructive towards making them healthy again. And when someone who had been very ill walked out of the ward, on their way back home, she would feel that everything she had done for them, be it only emptying bed-pans, making beds, or dusting lockers, had been infinitely worth while.

As the months went on, she learned more skills, was given more complex jobs to do, and gloried in these new abilities, gloried in the increasing responsibilities that they brought with them. Her only regret was that so few of the senior staff seemed to like her. When she was assigned to a new ward, she found the Sister there often cool, on one or two occasions actively hostile, and she could never understand this, for though she made no conscious efforts to please them, she knew her work to be well done. They *should* have liked her.

She would have been less surprised had she been able to listen to some of the gossipy conversations the Sisters indulged in in their sitting-room at nights. They talked about the nurses endlessly; and as a group, tended to form opinions based on others' experience and stick to them. And Sister Youngs, on Bridget's first ward, had disliked Bridget, said so loudly, and convinced all the others that the reserved, quiet girl wasn't just shy – which was the truth – but that her silence hid slyness, and that her watchful look was not born of interest in her work and concentration on it, but was rooted in a nasty sort of selfishness.

It was perhaps because of her awareness of the dislike she had engendered among the Sisters that she was so nervous now as she followed her friends along the corridor to Matron's Office. In a hospital the size of the Royal, the nurses saw Matron rarely – she had too little time to have close contact with her junior nurses she would have liked to have had. She depended heavily on the judgement of her Sisters, and Bridget knew this.

One by one, the nurses who were due to receive the striped belt that would proclaim the fact that they were now second-year nurses and had passed their preliminary exams, went into the office, and came out self-consciously smoothing the stiff, new belts round their middles. Liz and Judith and Bobby went in before Bridget, and while one other girl took her turn before Bridget herself, they stopped to whisper to her as she stood nervously waiting.

'She's a right old tartar,' Bobby giggled. 'Told me I'd scraped through by the merest fluke, and I'd have to wake my ideas up a bit before finals – but I don't much care. If you pass by a fluke or with flying colours, what's the odds? As long as you *get* through.'

'She doesn't miss much,' Liz said, blushing a little.

'Asked me if I was planning to get engaged or anything before finals – '

Judith grinned. 'She didn't ask me – how do you suppose she knows? I mean, that you and Ken are such love-birds, and that Bobby and me are playing the field?' For Judith, too, had boyfriends apart from Clive. 'Maybe she'll ask you if you're marrying David?' she said to Bridget, and grinned wickedly at Bridget's hot blush. 'I bet you do, for all you say you don't really like him. And he's not a bad catch, you know. Clive says he's got a private income and that's quite a thing – '

To Bridget's intense relief she didn't have to answer, for the other girl came out of the office and stood back to let Bridget take her place. And with her heart in her mouth, she walked in, crossed the wide expanse of carpet to the desk, and stood meekly in front of the woman sitting there with head bent over a folder of notes.

There was a short silence, in which Bridget found herself intensely aware of the distant sound of traffic from the main road far below, found herself stupidly counting the loud ticking that came from the clock on the mantelpiece.

'Sit down, Nurse Preston,' Matron said at length, and as Bridget obediently subsided into the hard chair at the front of the desk, looked at the apparently composed young face with a faint line between her brows.

'Are you happy here, Nurse?' she asked abruptly. 'Do you enjoy your work?'

'Yes, thank you, Matron,' Bridget said. Enjoy it? I wish I could explain how much, her thoughts murmured, but she said no more than that meek 'yes', which sounded unconvincing even in her own ears.

Matron leaned back, and looked across at her thoughtfully. 'You puzzle me, you know, Nurse Preston. Your examination results are uniformly excellent, your actual work on the wards appears to be satisfactory, yet somehow, the Sisters with whom you work find you – difficult, shall we say?'

'Difficult?' Bridget repeated, letting her eyes slide away from Matron's face, too shy, too nervous to look directly at her. Which was unfortunate, because it made Matron herself wonder if Bridget was sly, unable to meet her gaze because of a lack of honesty in her.

'A nurse needs sincerity, you know, Nurse Preston.' Matron's voice sharpened. 'Her first thoughts should be for her patients' welfare, not her own concerns. Some of the Sisters seem to feel that you are too wrapped up in yourself – that your good work is due not to a concern for patients' welfare but to a concern for your own needs. Is that true, would you say?'

No, no, her mind clamoured. It isn't. I'm just bad at talking to people, I can't make the Sisters understand that – I can talk to patients, but not to the Sisters – but all she said aloud was 'I don't know, Matron.'

'For Heaven's sake, girl – you ought to know! Do you think of your patients as you should, or don't you?'

'I – I try to, Matron,' Bridget said miserably. 'I try to. I – I like looking after them, truly I do – '

'Hmm.' Matron looked at her sharply. 'I realise that I have no right to interfere with your private life except inasmuch as it affects your work. But I gather you lead a – a fairly gay life, shall we say? I have often seen you and your friends at hospital parties and dances. I hope – I hope you are – sensible about your private relationships.'

Bridget felt her face go hot, and in an attempt to freeze her shaking lips into stillness set her face into a mould that looked to Matron to be decidedly mulish. Poor Bridget, with her positive gift for giving people the wrong impression. She wanted to please this woman very much indeed, respected her as a person and as the individual who was ultimately responsible for her work and welfare, and would have given anything to be able

80

to talk to her freely, to relax and tell her really how she felt. For a mad moment, she wondered if she could blurt out to Matron about her private difficulties, ask her how to tell David she didn't like him, how to tell Josh that she did, very much indeed, like him. But even as she thought it, she knew she couldn't and said only, 'I try to be sensible, Matron.'

The older woman sighed sharply, and leaned across her desk to pick up the striped belt that was ready for Bridget.

'Well, Nurse Preston, here is your belt. I must remind you that you have an even greater responsibility now that you have it, that patients will depend on you to a greater and greater extent, and that it is up to you to make yourself worthy of their dependence. Try to be – warmer, more thoughtful, and see if you can get better reports from the Sisters with whom you work from now on. Good afternoon, Nurse Preston.'

And Bridget almost stumbled from the room, clutching her belt in a cold hand.

She was glad the others had not waited for her, and went back across the courtyard to her room with her head whirling. It's not fair, she thought desperately, not fair. Why can't they understand, why can't any of them understand? I'm just not a person who can explain to people how I feel, I'm not made that way –

She locked herself in her room when she got there, to lie on her bed in the dusk of the early winter evening, to think and, to soothe her smarting feelings in privacy. Liz came and battered at her door and tried to open it, but she lay still, ignoring her. She heard Liz calling to the others that Bridget wasn't there, that she must have gone out somewhere, and Bobby's reply that she was going out with one of the new registrars, so she'd see Bridget in the morning, and Liz's footsteps clattered away down the corridor. Still Bridget lay on her bed, heard the other three chatter and giggle as they scampered in and out of each other's rooms to get ready to go out, heard the silence wash back into the building as they at last clattered away down the stairs towards their evenings out.

And as she lay there, long into the evening, her hands behind her head, staring at the dim square that was her window, she began to think about herself, about her relations with the three girls who were her friends, about David and Josh, about her work. Part of her knew perfectly well that in a way Liz and Judith and Bobby were bad for her. She had warmed to them first because they seemed to have all the qualities she herself lacked, and had wanted to be with them so that she could learn to be like them, warm and gay and friendly. Yet all that had happened was that she became, if anything, quieter, shyer, less capable of coping on her own, clinging to them as lifelines rather than because she really enjoyed their company – and then she pushed all her thoughts firmly to the back of her mind. It was no good thinking about it. I am as I am, she told herself and there it is.

They were put on night duty the next night, and for Bridget, this was an intense relief. Although Night Sister had a reputation of being a very stern woman, on night duty, one saw little of her – far less than one saw of a Sister on day duty.

She enjoyed night duty, the greater freedom to be with patients, the way she found herself doing complicated procedures that on day duty were done by third-year nurses, enjoyed being in charge of a ward at night, with a third-year nurse on call from a neighbouring ward for emergencies, and just a junior with her to cope with everything. She enjoyed the last round of the night, tucking patients down, turning off lights until only the shaded light over the desk in the centre was left to illuminate the big ward, enjoyed moving silently from bed to bed as the night wore on, checking that all the men in the ward were sleeping, giving warm drinks to the wakeful ones, even enjoyed the hectic rush of dressings, treatments, breakfasts, and bed-making that the morning brought. It was a male medical ward to which she had been assigned, and the work was heavy, many of the patients being old, needing a great deal of bedside nursing.

Everything seemed to be going very well, until she had been on the ward for about a month. She came on duty, a few days before Christmas, to find the Day Sister and nurses scurrying about busily. The Christmas decorations were already up, tinsel and paper chains swinging lazily from the light fittings, the huge Christmas tree sparkling with lights and coloured baubles, sprigs of holly and laurel drooping from the chart-racks above each bed. Some of the men, well enough to be up, were clustered round the big radiator, drinking some beer that Day Sister – a kindly woman – had allowed them 'because it was nearly Christmas'. But at the bed at the far end of the ward, there was a scurrying of nurses, screens pulled round to hide the patient from prying eyes, and a faint hiss of oxygen could be heard above the soft, murmuring voices of the other patients.

Bridget hurried down the ward to see what was going on while the junior set about the first jobs of the night, and slid round the screens to where Day Sister was leaning over the bed.

An oxygen tent was set up, translucent folds of polythene masking the occupant of the bed, the huge cylinder of oxygen beside him gleaming dully in the light.

Sister straightened, and nodded at Bridget. 'Evening, Nurse Preston. Hope you slept well,' her usual greeting, given with a sort of absence that made it clear that she was not really very interested.

'This man was picked up by the police down by the railways this afternoon. He's a tramp – very ill indeed. Clearly hasn't had much to eat for days, and Dr Winkworth thinks he's a meths drinker into the bargain.' She wrinkled her nose with distaste. 'He certainly smelled pretty ghastly when they brought him in. Anyway, he has lobar pneumonia – very nasty – both bases are completely full, by the sound of him, and his breathing is very poor indeed. Keep this oxygen going – there's plenty of ice in the cooling system, and see to it that you watch it carefully – it'll probably need renewing about midnight. He's on four-hourly tetracycline and you can give it straight into the drip.'

She indicated the tall stand beside the bed, where a bottle of glucose saline hung, red tubing running from it to the invisible arm inside the oxygen tent.

'Keep the glucose saline going, and watch him – I doubt he'll last the night, but he just might. There's a full cylinder of oxygen in the ante-room, though this'll last well into the small hours. All right?'

Bridget nodded, and watched Day Sister make the last check on the patient before following her out of the screens down to the desk to take the rest of the report.

'Half-hourly pulse on that man – don't know his name, by the way – no one's identified him yet, and I doubt very much if the police'll find anything about him – and keep an hourly blood-pressure chart, too. And an intake and output record. Right?'

She rattled through the rest of the report – and to Bridget's relief there was no other very ill patient in the ward, which meant she could concentrate on the pathetic wreck in bed seventeen – and pulled on her cuffs at last.

'I must go,' Sister said. 'There's a dress rehearsal for the Christmas show tonight, and I'm in it, God help me. Hope all goes well, Nurse – watch that man – and of course, you know about the general precautions? I've warned the men they mustn't smoke of course – see to it they don't. Don't want that tent going up in an explosion, do we? Though between ourselves, poor devil in it would hardly know if it did. He's right out. Anyway, I'm off. Goodnight,' and she bustled away, the last of the day nurses following her wearily.

Bridget hurried through the routine, settling the men, warning them again of the danger of smoking when there was highly inflammable oxygen in the ward, and when they were all settled, sent the junior to the kitchen to prepare the breakfast trolleys while she went up the ward to bed seventeen.

For the first time, she could see the patient inside the tent.

He was very old, his face deeply lined, the grooves in his sallow cheeks still showing dirt deeply ground in. Obviously, it would take a great deal of washing to get that out, she thought. And he was in no condition for such niceties. He was unshaven, the narrow cheeks covered with rough grey stubble, and his scrawny neck stuck out pathetically from the neck of the hospital's pyjama jacket. He lay with his head on one side, propped high on pillows, inside the tiny world of the oxygen tent, his lax lips crusted, his chest hardly moving as he breathed.

She slipped her hands carefully through the sleeves at the side of the tent, making sure that no oxygen escaped as she did so, and checked his pulse, made sure he had a clear airway, and with a sudden access of pity, stroked the grimy old face with a gentle finger.

Odd, she thought feeling something perilously close to tears in her throat. He was a baby once – it doesn't seem possible – such a wreck. I wonder what he was like when he was younger, why he's like this, who he belongs to, or who belongs to him –

But the old man just lay mutely, his closed eyes deep

85

in his dirty thin face, the hollowing of the temples that indicated the severity of his condition making his head look skull-like.

And then, sighing sharply, she sealed the tent again, checked the cylinder and the ice, and began to enter the readings of his blood pressure and pulse on to his chart.

As she finished, and hung the chart back at the foot of the bed, she raised her head sharply, and sniffed. There was no mistake about it – she could smell cigarette smoke, somewhere near.

Moving with all the speed she had, she came out of the screens, and peered round the ward. The men were all lying humped in their beds, apparently snoring, and she could see no tell-tale glow – and then, a tall figure appeared at the end of the ward, silhouetted against the light. As it came towards her, she, too, hurried towards it, for she could see the bright glow of a cigarette held in its hand. I must put a notice at the door for the doctors, she thought anxiously, and then, she was face to face with the man who was smoking.

'Hello,' he said, his voice thick and blurred. ' 'S'me – David. How're you, sweetheart?'

She peered up at him in the darkness, and whispered sharply, 'David – I've got an oxygen tent going – put that cigarette out – ' and she reached for it.

He laughed, loudly, so that one or two of the men stirred in their sleep, and teasingly held the cigarette high out of her reach. 'Whatsamatter, lovey? Want to smoke?'

'Give me that, you idiot,' she said, louder now, her voice thin with her fear for the oxygen she could hear still hissing behind her. 'I've got a tent up, don't you understand?'

'Aha!' And he laughed again. 'Florence Nightingale on the warpath – scared there'll be an accident?'

'Of course I am!' She was nearly crying now. 'Are you too drunk to care, you lunatic?' for he was obviously very drunk indeed.

'Got it in one, sweetheart. Been a nice big party in the mess, and I'm as sloshed as a newt – ' and he raised his other hand high, and she could see the light glint on a half full glass in it.

Almost sick with terror now, she did the only thing she could do. She turned him by sheer force, propelled him as fast as she could down the ward towards the doors at the end, while he slithered on the polished floor in front of her. They reached the door, and there he set himself against the jamb, and managed to stop her headlong rush.

'Now go easy, sweetheart,' he said, his voice ugly suddenly. 'I only came to say hello to you, give you a nice Christmas kiss – '

He lurched towards her suddenly, just as she managed at last to wrench the cigarette from his hand, and as he lurched the glass in his hand fell tinkling to the floor, to splash her apron as it went. She smelled the thick reek of whisky, as she ground the cigarette out. And then, off her guard, his arms were round her, and he was pushing her head back in a violent kiss that hurt her mouth, that made her head swim with the fumes of the whisky he had been drinking. He pulled at her uniform, so that her collar burst open under his onslaught, and the bib of her apron tore from the pins that held it to her dress, and her cap fell to the floor as he tried to run one hand through her hair.

'Stop it, you idiot – stop it – ' She managed to get her hand away from his, tried desperately to pull right away from him.

And then, suddenly, he pulled away from her himself, and stood awkwardly straightening his tie as he stared over her shoulder.

She turned herself, fumbling with her collar, agonisingly aware of the torn apron she was wearing, the stain of whisky on her skirt, her cap lying at her feet, to see Night Sister staring at her with a face rigid with shock, blue eyes icy with rage.

Chapter 8

David seemed to have been shocked into sobriety by Night Sister's sudden appearance.

'Evening, Sister,' he said, and his voice sounded almost normal, though there was still a faint blur about the sibilants. 'Just going – ' and he made a move towards the main outer doors of the ward, while Bridget stood in dumb misery, trying to do up her collar, fumbling with the pins on her torn apron.

'I'd like to speak to you, if you don't mind, Dr Nestor,' Sister said, not taking her eyes from Bridget. 'You will wait for me, please – outside the ward,' and meekly, David nodded, and with a quick glance at Bridget, slid out of the little group and went to the door. As it swished shut behind him, Night Sister said to Bridget, 'Where is your Junior?'

'In – in the kitchen, Sister – laying the trolleys for – '

Night Sister pushed the kitchen door open, and called the junior out. 'Go into the ward, Nurse,' she said curtly, 'and stay there until I tell you what to do,' and with a startled look at the dishevelled Bridget, the junior scuttled into the dimness of the big ward.

'Now, Nurse, come in here. Tidy yourself up at once.'

Under Night Sister's icy-blue gaze, Bridget started to tidy her uniform, to set her crumpled cap back on her head, and when she had managed to make some semblance of order, stood still to wait for the onslaught of Night Sister's tongue.

There was a long pause, and then Night Sister said, her voice thin with controlled anger, 'Now, perhaps, you can offer some explanation of that disgraceful scene?'

Bridget took a deep breath, and swallowed hard. She was shaking with reaction, with tears very near the surface, and for one ghastly moment, as she opened and closed her mouth, she thought she wouldn't be able to speak at all.

'He – he was smoking,' she managed at last. 'Smoking. And there's a tent up. I was frightened. And he wouldn't – he wouldn't put it out. I *had* to make him put it out – there was oxygen – '

'Well? That still doesn't explain what I saw, does it?'

'He wouldn't put it out,' Bridget said desperately. 'He just wouldn't. And – and when I took it away from him, he – he – ' but she couldn't go on.

'Is Dr Nestor a friend of yours?' There was a world of scorn in the way Night Sister said the word 'friend', a scorn that made Bridget squirm sickly. A friend of hers? How could she possibly explain the relationship that existed between her and David, the unwillingness she felt towards that relationship, the reasons for its continued existence? She couldn't. All she could say was, 'A – sort of friend, I suppose – a sort of friend.'

'I can imagine what sort,' and now Sister was really sneering. 'I can well imagine. However, that is no concern of mine. You can explain the rest to Matron in the morning. In the meantime, since you are clearly not to be trusted in charge of a ward, you had better spend the rest of the night in Casualty where Staff Nurse can keep an eye on you, and I will send someone else here. And you will go to Matron as soon as you are off duty in the morning, do you understand? Go to Casualty now, and ask Staff Nurse to send Nurse Jessolo here to take over from you. And keep out of my sight for the rest of the night. I don't want to see you – you make me *sick*!' and she held the kitchen door open for Bridget to pass her.

Outside the ward, David was leaning against the wall, obediently waiting for Night Sister, and as Bridget went past him, he put a hand out to stop her. But she looked at him with such anger, such loathing in her face, that even he, unperceptive as he was, dropped his hand in confusion, and let her go.

The rest of the night dragged for Bridget. A curious Night Staff Nurse, down in Casualty, tried to get her to explain why she had been banished from her ward. But Bridget only shook her head, and refused to talk, which annoyed the Staff Nurse enough to make her send Bridget to the sluice to spend the long, dark hours cleaning equipment and making dressings ready to be packed in the big drums for the morning.

There were not even any accidents during the night to break the monotony, to keep the department and Bridget busy, so she had nothing to keep her thoughts from their sick repetition of anger, of fear and a sort of shame. She knew perfectly well that it had been David's fault that the whole thing had happened. He had been drunk, and behaved outrageously. But part of her mind kept reminding her that he would never have behaved so if it had not been for the relationship between them, the memory of the hours she had spent necking with him. He had every right to expect her to behave as badly as he had himself, she told herself miserably. Every right.

The long night came to an end at last, and Bridget dragged her aching and miserable body to Night Nurses' supper at nine in the morning, to sit next to the other three, trying to eat the cold meat pie and boiled potatoes and cabbage the hospital provided for this dull meal. Already, she discovered, everyone on night duty knew what had happened. The junior on the male

91

medical ward had overheard Night Sister talking to
David, after Bridget's departure for Casualty, and had
lost no time in recounting – not without embellishment –
the details of the whole sordid business as she knew it.

Bobby was highly amused by it all, though Liz was
sympathetic. Judith, as usual, simply followed Bobby's
lead, and laughed at Bridget's misery with her.

'Oh, come off it, Bridie!' Bobby said at length, staring
at Bridget over the rim of her coffee cup as they finished
their meal. 'Why all the glummery? So you got copped
having a quiet snog – you aren't the first, and you won't
be the last. Matron'll give you a bit of a nagging, and
that'll be that! No need to behave as though the world
had come to an end! Cheer up, love!'

'Oh, leave her alone, Bobby,' Liz said, uncomfortably, looking at Bridget as she sat slumped dumbly in
her chair, her untouched food in front of her. 'I'd be
scared too. You know what a tongue Matron's got –
and I bet it wasn't Bridget's fault, anyway – was it,
Bridie?'

Bridget looked up at her and said quietly, 'No it
wasn't – ' and she warmed to Liz, managing a smile
at the friendly face across the table.

And then, it was time to go to Matron's Office. She
stood outside the door, hearing the faint sound of Night
Sister's voice inside as she gave the night report, seeing
the morning bustle about her with unseeing eyes, but
aware of the incongruity of the Christmas decorations
that bedecked the long corridor, of the chilliness of the
wintry morning.

Night Sister came out of the office, and stood back,
grimfaced and tight-lipped, to let Bridget go in, and
summoning all the strength she had, Bridget walked
across the carpeted floor to stand in front of the big
desk at the far end of the room.

Matron looked up at her, and at the sight of the
pinched, white face, the misery in the big, grey eyes,

much of the anger that Night Sister's account of the night's happenings had roused in her dissipated. She had expected to meet – dumb insolence perhaps, a perky insouciance, regret at having been caught rather than regret that the episode had happened at all. But this girl was clearly deeply unhappy, terrified, and Matron, instead of showing the anger with which she had intended to speak, smiled at Bridget, and said gently, 'Sit down, Nurse Preston.'

Her gentleness was too much for Bridget. She stared at the older woman, and then, the tears that had been so near the surface all night at last broke bounds, and came tumbling down her face, filling her throat and nose with tight misery, so that all she could do was collapse into the proffered chair, and bury her head in shaking hands.

Matron said nothing, letting the storm subside, and gradually Bridget brought herself under control again, and wiping her eyes to a puffy redness, at last sat silent, head bowed in front of the big desk.

'Now, Nurse Preston. Tell me what happened last night. And why it happened. Because that is what really matters.'

Bridget took a deep and shuddering breath. 'Dr – Dr Nestor came to the ward last night,' she began. 'And he was smoking. I could smell it. And – there was an oxygen tent up, and I was frightened.' She looked at the older woman who just nodded encouragingly. 'I told Dr Nestor – about the tent – but – but' – she wanted to say, 'he was too drunk to care – too drunk' but this was impossible. For all her anger towards David, she knew that to say he was drunk and came to a ward would get him into very severe trouble indeed, and a streak of loyalty in her made it impossible to pile any more on to David than she had to. So she said, 'I – I don't think he understood – not properly. Anyway, I took it away from him, and put it out. And then – then – '

93

Just as when she had tried to explain to Night Sister, she balked at this point, but Matron just raised her eyebrows at her, and sat silently, clearly waiting for her to go on. So she tried again.

'He – it was Christmas, he said.' Perhaps the fact that it was Christmas would constitute some sort of excuse. 'And – and he – well, he grabbed me, and – and he' – she closed her eyes and swallowed. 'I tried to stop him, really I did. But – he's very strong.' As she said it, she could feel the almost brute strength of his arms round her. 'And when I tried to stop him – my apron got torn, and – everything. And then Night Sister came,' her voice trailed away into silence.

Matron stirred. 'That is what happened,' she said at last. 'But not *why*. When I talked to you a few weeks ago, when you got your second-year belt, I asked you then if you were – sensible about your private life. This episode – this shows that perhaps you are not as sensible as you might be.'

Bridget said nothing, just sitting staring at her hands clasped on her lap.

'Look, Nurse Preston. I know perfectly well that young women like you need boy-friends. I know how much it matters to you to have a boy-friend. But let me assure you that there is no need for any girl to – put up with the attentions of a man she does not really care for just for the sake of having such a boy-friend. Do you understand what I mean?'

Bridget raised her head and looked at her. 'I – it isn't that I specially want to – to – '

'There are plenty of other people around from whom you can choose friends, you know. If you don't really care for this man, and he does not really care for you – and I can't think that he really does, for if he did, he would never have allowed last night's scene to happen – '

But Bridget, to her own amazement, interrupted.

'How do you know I don't really – like him?' she asked wonderingly.

Matron laughed at this. 'My dear child, I am not nearly as stupid as some of you girls think I am. I am not a Matron of a hospital like this one as – as a freak of nature, you know. I *do* know something about people, about their needs, and behaviours, and listening to you explain what happened last night makes it clear – to me at any rate – that this Dr Nestor is not someone for whom you care very deeply. I suspect that – that your friendship is something that happened to you, and that it is not one you sought for yourself.'

Bridget nodded miserably, 'Yes – ' she murmured. 'Yes.'

'I am beginning to realise that you are a person to whom things happen, Nurse Preston. You are not – not fully in control of your life, shall we say?'

Bridget nodded again, and at the warmth in the face across the desk said breathlessly. 'That's exactly it, Matron, really it is. I'm – I'm not very used to people – ' She stopped, and then said with a sort of ruefulness, 'I never really had the chance to learn how – '

Matron nodded. 'And you let other people push you about – even get the wrong impression of you, and you do nothing about it – the Sisters think you are silent because of insolence. That you are self-absorbed. Are you?'

'Oh, no, Matron, really I'm not,' Bridget said eagerly. 'I – I'm just not good at – well, explaining to people. So I don't try. And then – then – '

'Then they don't try to understand *you*,' Matron finished. 'Now listen to me, Nurse Preston. You are not a child. You are a grown woman, nearly. And you must learn how to control your own life. You must not let events and people take hold of you. Do you understand that? If a particular friend seems, after you have known him for a while, to be the wrong friend for you, then do something about the situation. Don't just drift. This time, it is all right. I can see that what happened was not entirely your fault – except inasmuch as you *should* have been in better control of matters than you were – so we will say no more about it. But I shall be more than disappointed in you if you allow such an episode to happen again. Do you understand? I am not going to tell you to break off a friendship if you do not want to – I have no right to do so. But if I hear that you are still drifting, as you clearly have been, I will suspect that you are not fit to continue to train at the Royal. A girl who cannot control her own life will never make a nurse. Now go to bed, and come on duty tonight ready to make a new start. I will explain matters satisfactorily to Night Sister – but it is up to you to convince her that you are to be trusted in future.'

Bridget got to her feet, smoothing her apron in front of her. 'Thank you, Matron,' she said. 'Thank you – ' For a moment, she wanted to explain to Matron that it wasn't because she just wanted to have a boy-friend that she put up with David. That it was because she needed other friends – and that without a willingness to be David's friend, she feared that the other three would shut her out – and that it was that that mattered to her. But already Matron was reaching for the pile of paper work on her desk, and Bridget allowed her inherent diffidence to override her need to explain.

Outside the office door, she leaned against the wall for a moment, trying to collect her thoughts. The darkness behind her closed eyes swirled momentarily, and she took a deep breath before opening them.

And as she opened them, and stood straight, she saw Josh standing in front of her, his friendly face smiling a little, his head on one side as he looked at her.

'Hello, Tiddler,' he said gently. 'On the carpet?'

At the sight of him, her still very shaky control slipped again, and to her horror, she found tears welling up into her eyes again. Josh's own face altered at the sight of her distress, and with a quick movement, he took her arm, and hurried her away down the corridor.

'Come on, Tiddler. Can't have you weeping all over the place – come and tell your Uncle Josh all about it – ' and he led her towards the hospital coffee shop, while she tried desperately to push her tears back down inside her again.

He chattered cheerfully as he settled her at the table in the corner, giving her time to regain control, and she was grateful to him for his quick understanding. Then, when they were settled with steaming cups in front of them, he leaned forwards and smiled at her.

'Was it that business last night the old girl was wigging you about Tiddler?'

She looked at him quickly, and then dropped her eyes to her cup.

'Yes – ' she said in a low voice. 'And she was right, really.'

'David should have been shot, the idiot. He was drunk as a lord, and he shouldn't have come anywhere near the wards in that state.'

'I know,' Bridget said wearily. 'But he did.'

'Did – did you tell the old girl he was drunk?'

She shook her head. 'I thought there'd be a row for him if I did.'

'You're damn' right there – he'd have had the book thrown at him.' Josh looked at her sharply. 'You're a good lass, Tiddler. Old David doesn't know how lucky he is, I reckon. There aren't many who'd carry the can back like you've done.'

She shrugged. 'It doesn't matter,' she said, and suddenly felt desperately weary. 'It doesn't matter.'

'But he is lucky,' Josh said softly, and put a hand out towards her. 'Any man with a girl like you to care for him is lucky, you know that?'

She looked up at him, at the face that was so achingly

familiar, and all the feeling she had for him suddenly bubbled up inside her so that her mouth trembled, and her eyes brimmed with tears again. She put her hands in her lap, to avoid his touch, feeling that the warmth of his hand on hers would be more than she could cope with.

'I – I don't care for him,' she said baldly. 'I – don't. I – hate him.'

He looked at her uncertainly for a moment. 'Hate him? I thought – you said once that – I don't understand. You've been going about with him for a long time, Tiddler. Or is it just that now you're angry with him? You've every right to be.'

'I – it was – ' She took a deep breath. 'It just happened. I never did specially care for him. Not really. He was – just one of the crowd.'

'Oh, for God's sake, Bridget!' He sounded angry suddenly. 'Don't tell me you just went around with a man out of habit – I don't believe it. Some girls would – but you?'

'Well, it's true.' She hated herself then, hated her own weakness. 'The others – they got mad if I said I didn't want to go out with David – so I did. That's all there ever was to it. I never want to see him again – and I don't care what the others say. I just don't care – '

'Did it matter so much to you?' he asked curiously. 'What the other girls said?'

'I never – I never had friends before them,' Bridget said softly, 'and they were such fun, and so gay – I – I wanted to be like them. But – well, I was wrong. I'm just not like them, and I never will be. I – I guess they'll have to take me as I am. If they don't like me that way, that's all there is to it.'

He sat in silence for a moment. Then he said gently, 'Tiddler – tell me something. If you don't care for David Nestor, is there anyone else you care about? Anyone at all?'

She looked up at him, at his warm smile, at the deep clefts in his cheeks, and every fibre of her ached to say 'Yes – yes. I care for you – for you.' The words trembled on her lips for a brief second and then, across the crowded coffee shop, she saw Bobby appear at the door, her fair hair swinging over the thick sweater and tight trousers she had changed into.

The words died unspoken, and she sat in silence as Bobby saw them, and came swinging over towards them.

'Hello, Bridie, my love. Hello, Josh, my angel,' and she dropped a casual kiss on to Josh's head as she slid into the vacant chair beside them. 'So what happened, Bridie? Did the old girl have your guts for garters? Old David had a hell of a pasting from Night Sister. She threatened to tell the Chief of Staff all about his wicked ways, but he persuaded her to show a little of the milk of human kindness – poor old David – he's feeling awful about it all this morning.' She laughed then. 'He's got the father and mother of a hangover, and he's been looking everywhere for you to apologise, and he couldn't find you. He's on his way to a clinic now, so he'll have to wait to make his peace with you till later. I just met him in the courtyard.'

'I don't – I don't want to see him, not now or later,' Bridget said, her voice low, but firm. 'I just don't want to see him.'

Bobby hitched her chair closer to Josh, and linked an arm through his, and winked at him. But he was looking at Bridget and made no response.

'Don't be nasty to him, Bridget!' Bobby said. 'He didn't mean to get you into hot water – put it down to your lovely eyes. He just wanted his Bridget, I suppose.'

'Stop it, Bobby!' Bridget said violently. 'I tell you I never want to talk to him again. I've had enough, do you understand? Enough.'

Bobby frowned sharply. 'Oh, come off it, Bridget. No need for all the dramatics. So you got caught necking! So what? The old girl hasn't fired you, has she?'

'No – but that's got nothing to do with it. Nothing at all. I'm – I'm finished, that's all. Finished,' and she felt a wave of relief wash over her as she said it.

'Give the poor old devil a chance, Bridget!' Bobby said. 'Look, he just wants to apologise, that's all. It's not fair not to let him, is it? Listen, Bridie' – she leaned over the table – 'we've all got nights off next weekend – and Ken and Clive and Josh are off too – I've already arranged it, haven't I Josh? We're going down to my people's place for the weekend – a real breath of clean air and peace, down in the country. And I just asked David, and he says he'll come, as long as you do. Now, please, Bridie – don't spoil things for everyone – it's all fixed, eh, Josh ? We'll have a ball, and a real rest, and it'll be fun. Now don't be difficult Bridie – nothing to get difficult about. Come down with us, and give old David another chance.'

Bridget looked up at her, at her wheedling face, and then at Josh, still sitting silently across the table, and felt all her newfound resolve crumbling in her, as it always did when she was faced with Bobby's charm.

'I don't want to, Bobby,' she said with a sort of desperation – and knew as she said it that it was no use. 'I'd rather not, truly.'

And then Josh leaned forwards, and smiled at her. 'Listen, Tiddler, Bobby has got a point, you know. Even if you really are going to give David the push, you ought to tell him so. You can't just – disappear. Not in a place like this. If you're going to do it, do it clean. Come down for the weekend with us. And then start from scratch.'

Bridget looked from face to face, and then closed her eyes in sudden weariness. 'All right. I'll come. But that's it. Never again after that. I've had enough.'

'Good girl,' Josh said softly, and then with a quick glance at Bobby closed his mouth firmly. And Bobby grinned triumphantly and said cheerfully, 'You'll change your mind, love. You see if you don't. David's a nice old thing, really – just gets a bit wild sometimes. You'll change your mind.'

And Bridget took herself off to bed, leaving Josh and Bobby in the coffee shop, her last sight of them sitting close together making her grateful Bobby had come in time to prevent her making a complete fool of herself. For she was sure, seeing them together, that they were meant to be together, that her own feeling for Josh must never be allowed to show itself. Josh and Bobby belonged together, and there was nothing Bridget could do about it.

Chapter 9

She managed to avoid seeing David at all for the rest of that week. He had more sense than to come to her ward at night, keeping well out of Night Sister's way, and Bridget made sure she avoided all the places where he might be during the day, refusing to join the others for morning coffee in the coffee shop, going straight to her room and bed as soon as she came off duty. Bobby and Liz and Judith, with a rare tact, said nothing to her about what had happened, only chattering of their plans for the Christmas weekend they were to spend at Bobby's home.

There was one bad moment for Bridget, at supper one morning when, listening to the others, she discovered that the weekend was not to be spent, as she assumed, in the company of Bobby's parents. They were away on a winter cruise, and when Bridget heard this, she said baldly that she wasn't going.

But Bobby was angered by her demurs. 'For Christ's sake, Bridget, what's the matter with you? You aren't going on a dirty weekend or anything! There's to be eight of us – eight of us! No one's asking you to do anything you shouldn't! We've a big place – and everyone's got a room of his and her own! I'm not running a – a bawdy house, you know!' and she looked so indignant at the implied insult Bridget had offered her that Bridget perforce gave in.

'Anyway, it's the last time,' she told herself firmly, as she packed a case for the weekend. 'If Bobby and

Liz and Judith decide to do without me, that's too bad. After this weekend, I'm on my own. I'll do what I want to do when I want to do it, and that's that. I *will* control my own life – after this weekend.'

It was a lovely house. Bridget had always known that Bobby's parents were rich, but she had not expected anything quite as beautiful as the country house in front of which the two cars drew up after the two-hour drive from London. It had been a silent journey for Bridget, in David's company for the first time since the episode in the ward. She and Bobby and David had travelled down in Josh's car, while the others came in Ken's, and she had sat in stony silence next to David all the way. He, after one look at her face, had made no attempt to speak to her or touch her, and she was grateful for this, at least.

The house was an old one, with rambling corridors, unexpected steps up and down in odd corners, and big, comfortably furnished rooms. As Bobby had promised, each of them had a room of their own, Bridget being allotted Bobby's old nursery, while the men were accommodated in the four maids' bedrooms at the top of the house.

'The folks only have a housekeeper these days,' Bobby said gaily, as she showed them all round. 'And a couple of dailies from the town. But they're all on holiday too, so we'll have to fend for ourselves. More fun, anyway. Can you cook, Josh?'

'Like an angel,' he assured her, cheerfully. 'I'm a dab hand with a boiled egg, I promise you!'

'Some Christmas dinner that'll be!' Bobby jeered. 'I've ordered a flipping great turkey from the farm – so someone'll have to cook it – '

'I can cook,' Ken said unexpectedly, 'and with Liz to peel the vegetables, you'll get a meal fit for a king,' and he kissed Liz resoundingly. 'She'll have to learn sooner or later – if she's going to marry me, what say you, Liz?'

and Liz laughed and blushed a little and looked up at him adoringly.

And even now that they were all at the house, Bridget managed to keep out of David's way. They unpacked their clothes, and all went down to the local pub for a drink, filling the small country bar with noise and laughter, so that the regulars looked across at them with indulgent grins, and joined in the teasing of Liz and Ken, neither of whom minded the laughter a bit. Only Bridget, sitting as far away from David as she could, and David himself, were quiet. But Bridget could not help noticing that David was, as usual, drinking a great deal more than was good for him, while she sat with the same untouched drink for the whole evening.

When the pub closed, the eight of them went singing back through the dark wintry lanes, and Bridget, the only one not merry from the effects of the drinks they had had, listened to them and watched them with a sort of cool surprise.

'I can't think what it was I saw in them all,' she told herself wonderingly. 'Ken and Liz – they're nice. I could have been Liz's friend anyway, and she wouldn't have demanded so much from me. But Bobby and Judith – they – I don't even *like* them – '

She looked across at Bobby as they arrived at the house, dropping coats and gloves in a disorderly pile in the big hall, collapsing laughing and shouting in the big armchairs in the drawing room. Bobby, her fair face flushed with excitement and drink, sprawled across a somehow quiet Josh, a Josh who seemed to Bridget to have only a surface gaiety tonight, lacking the sparkle and warmth that he usually had, seeming to force his jokes and laughter. She looked at Bobby, and wondered at herself.

The fascination that had held Bridget so firmly for this past year seemed to disappear suddenly, to melt like snow in a morning's bright sunshine. She was noisy, she was gay – but she was shallow, Bridget told herself. She gives nothing but a spurious friendship, but she takes everything everyone has to offer. And with a flash of insight, Bridget realised suddenly that Bobby was essentially a very lonely person, even lonelier than Bridget herself. For Bridget at least realised that she was lonely, that she needed friendship. Bobby doesn't know, Bridget told herself. She doesn't know a thing about herself.

With a sigh, Bridget left the others to wander off in search of the kitchen. She needed coffee, and so did the others, even if they didn't realise it. She found the kitchen at the back of the house, and rooted in cupboards and drawers for the equipment to make black coffee for them all. She took her time, in no hurry to return to the others, and when the kettle boiled, poured the steaming water over the coffee grounds; and filled cups on a tray.

It wasn't until she had made her careful way, with her loaded tray, back to the drawing-room, that she realised that silence had descended on the big house. She put the tray down on a low table near the door and straightened up to peer into the dimly lit room.

Only one light was burning, a small table-lamp, and the only other source of light was from the logs burning with uneasily flickering flames in the wide, brick fireplace. For a moment, she thought the room was empty, and told herself ruefully, 'I've made all that coffee for nothing,' not stopping to wonder why the others had gone. And, then as she turned to pick up her own cup, a movement in the shadows brought her whirling round.

David was sitting sprawled in an armchair by the fire, his head slumped deep into his shoulders, his brooding eyes staring out at her from his silent face. She looked at him for a moment, and then turned away, meaning to go to bed.

But he stood up, and came round in front of her, barring her way to the door.

'I want to talk to you,' he said, and his voice was thick.

'I'm afraid I don't want to talk to you, David,' Bridget's own calmness almost surprised her. 'There's nothing to say.'

'Oh, yes, there is,' he said, and came closer, so that she could smell the whisky on his breath. Uncertainly, she stepped back, and said again, with rather less conviction, 'I don't want to talk to you, David. Not now, or ever.'

'What'sa matter with you, for Christ's sake? What you coming the prude for all of a sudden?' He sounded angry, his voice thick and blurred. 'A year you've been going around with me – a year! And now all of a sudden, you don't want to know! So there was a row at the hospital – !' His voice changed suddenly, became placatory. 'Look, I'm sorry about that, I was drunk, and I don't deny it, and I got you into a row, and you covered up for me, and I'm damned grateful. I'm ready to apologise – really I am – no need to get all chilly and nasty, is there?' and he put his hands out to grasp her arms.

She shrank back from him, now frankly loathing the thought of his touch, no longer able to merely tolerate him.

'Keep away from me! I tell you I don't want to talk to you. The only reason I agreed to come here this weekend was so that I could finish all this. I don't want to talk to you now or ever. You've apologised. All right. I accept your apology, and all I want from now is to be left alone – just to be left alone – '

'What's the matter with you?' he said, angry again. 'Why the prudery all of a sudden? You came down here for the same reason the rest of us did – and don't go getting girlish and pretending otherwise – I don't fall for that sort of guff, do you hear? All right. I behaved badly, and I said I was sorry, and I am, if it got you into trouble, so let's forget it now, and have some fun – come on – ' and he lurched towards her, so that she had to back away from him if she was to avoid him.

He was really furious now, his eyes blazing in his white face, and as he forced her back into the hall beyond the big drawing-room doors, she felt real fear bubbling up inside her.

'Keep away from me – keep away from me!' she said, her voice cracking a little, her eyes wide with terror. 'Don't touch me – don't – '

But he was too quick for her, and his arms, the arms whose strength she had fought in the past, were round her, and his whisky-reeking breath hot on her face. She squirmed, twisting her head away from his face, but he put a steely hand under her chin and forced her head back, his own face coming closer. She did the only thing she could do – turned her head sharply and bit his hand hard, so that he yelped with the pain, and in a sudden rage, pulled his arm back and hit her, so that her face stung, and her head whipped back on her neck with a sharp crack that made her whole body hurt.

'You little bitch!' he said, and his voice was now without the blur of drink. 'You bitch! Stringing me along like some – if you think you're getting away with that, you're mistaken – ' and once again he made a grab for her, this time pulling at her thin dress so that it ripped right away from her shoulder.

She struggled, heard her own voice shouting, heard herself almost screaming with fear, and then, suddenly, there was a clatter of feet on the stairs, a rush of light as someone put on a switch upstairs, and she felt, rather than saw, someone pull David away from her.

'What in God's name are you doing, you lunatic!' It was Josh. Josh, in a dressing-gown pulled untidily round him, his usually neat hear ruffled above his wide face.

108

He was holding on to David from behind, both arms held tightly, while David tried to pull away from him.

'You keep out of this, Simpson!' David shouted, managing to get out of Josh's firm grip, to turn and glare at him. 'This is none of your bloody business!'

'What's going on down there?' Bobby's voice came coolly from the head of the stairs, and Bridget looked up to see her standing there, a thin dressing-gown pulled negligently round her, her bare legs under its shortness making it obvious she was wearing nothing else.

David looked up at her, and laughed loudly, without humour. 'What's going on? What's going on? Your *friend* here has decided she doesn't like the idea of this weekend after all – changed her mind. She knows bloody well why we're here, and now she doesn't want to play. And your boy-friend has decided to muscle in on what doesn't concern him – that's what's happening – '

'It does concern me,' Josh said, his voice very even. 'A private argument becomes public property when you can hear it for miles around – and if – if Bridget didn't need help, she wouldn't have screamed like that.'

Bridget was leaning against the staircase now, clutching at her torn dress, still shaking with fright as she stared at the two angry men, and as the other four, hearing the row, appeared at the top of the stairs, she shrank even closer to the stairs. Bad enough Josh had to hear what David was saying, without everyone else being an audience. But David had no such qualms. He was shouting again.

'Don't be so bloody sanctimonious, Simpson! You've got what you want, haven't you? You came down here for the same reason I did – you've got a willing girl, so never mind anyone else, is that it? It's all right for you to have a toss, but hard luck on anyone else with a girl that isn't quite so accommodating! After the last year, believe me, I've got every right to get mad – she's no more than a – '

'Watch it, Nestor – ' Josh cut in sharply before David could finish his sentence. 'You're drunk, and you don't know what you're saying – '

'I know what I'm saying all right, believe me I do. She's been playing me for a complete idiot, and she isn't going to get away with it!'

'Listen, you damned idiot!' Josh shouted at him. 'Drunk you may be, but it doesn't mean *you* can get away with anything you want to! Be your age, man!'

'Oh, Josh, for Heaven's sake!' Bobby came down the stairs, her face creased with irritation. 'Leave them alone. What's it got to do with us, for God's sake? Bridget's a big girl – she can look after herself. Come back upstairs, and leave them to sort out their own arguments.'

'Yes, why don't you?' David said, sneering. 'Your girl's all ready and waiting for you. Why not leave me to sort out mine?'

And now Bridget managed to move. 'There's nothing to sort out,' she said dully. 'I'm sorry, Bobby. Sorry for the noise. I'll leave now. I'm going back to London,' and she moved towards the stairs, grateful for the way Josh moved forwards to cover her from David as she did so.

But David made no move to touch her, this time. 'You go,' he said shortly. 'You go. I wouldn't want you if you were the last female going, believe me. You go running back to London and find another mug to play your pretty games with,' and he pushed past Josh and went back to the drawing-room to pour himself another drink at the bar in the corner.

Bridget dragged herself up the stairs, past Liz and Judith, both standing with Clive and Ken, staring at her. Bobby stood back as she passed her, and said

110

shortly, 'Well, I hope you're satisfied. You've ruined everyone's weekend, you with all your fuss.'

And now Bridget, almost for the first time in her life, lost her temper.

'I didn't want to come – you know I didn't!' she said, blazing at Bobby. 'When I heard your parents were not going to be here, I said I didn't want to come, and you said it was all right! All right! You – you're as bad as he is, do you know that? You've got the morals of – of a tom-cat, and I was a fool not to see it sooner! You sleep around if you want to – that's your business! But don't try to make me do the same! I'm going back to London, and I never want to speak to you again – ' and she pulled away, and ran up the stairs towards her room.

Liz followed her, and stood hesitantly at the door as Bridget, moving as fast as she could, changed her dress, and threw her things into her suitcase.

'I'm sorry about this, Bridget,' she said, her voice ashamed. 'I – I thought you knew, really – I didn't know you truly didn't like David – '

'Whether I like him or not hasn't anything to do with it. I'd need to feel rather more than that to – to spend this sort of weekend with him – ' Bridget said roughly.

Liz winced at that, and went a hot red. 'It's different for me and Ken,' she said, her voice almost apologetic. 'I mean, I'm not like Bobby and Judith. They're fun to be with, so I – well, I strung along. But Ken and I are going to be married soon and – and well, we don't get a chance to – to be together much really. So we came. But we aren't like them – '

'It doesn't matter,' Bridget said, closing her case, and shrugging her coat on. 'It doesn't matter. I was a damned fool not to see what the set-up was long ago. Well, now I know. Leave it at that,' and she pushed past Liz, and went purposefully down the stairs.

The drawing-room door was shut and she breathed

111

a sigh of relief at that. She wouldn't have to see David again, at least. Josh was sitting on the bottom step, and she went past him without a word.

'I persuaded you to come,' he said in a low voice. 'I should have known better. I'm sorry.'

She stopped by the front door, and said without turning, 'There's no need for you to apologise. I should have known myself. And thank you for – for your help.'

He came and stood beside her, putting a hand on her arm.

'Please, Bridget. Can I tell you something? Why I wanted you to come here this weekend?'

'I've told you it doesn't matter,' she said dully.

'It matters to me,' he said. 'Listen. I – I've always liked you, you know. I said you were different, and so you are. You're sweet, and innocent – '

'Innocent!' She laughed shortly at that. 'Innocent! Ignorant and stupid, and pushed any way anyone wants to push me – '

'No,' he said softly. 'Innocent. That's why this happened, really. And I respect that in you. Very much. I'd hoped that this weekend – well, that I'd be able to find out for certain whether you cared for David – whether it was anger that made you say you hated him, or whether you meant it. It – it mattered to me to find out. Do you understand what I'm saying?'

She turned and looked at him then, and her grey eyes were level in their gaze.

'I thought you had come for the same reason everyone else seems to have come here. For – for cheap sex, for "fun", for a "giggle" – ' she said evenly.

He reddened. 'I deserve that, I suppose.'

'Don't you? Are you trying to say that you came here for any other reason. As David said – Bobby is ready and willing. Why don't you go and find her? She'll –

112

she'll be getting angry, no doubt.' And she was amazed at the cold anger in her own voice.

'Listen to me,' he said, his voice hard and even. 'I can't deny that I've been having – "fun" as you put it, with Bobby. For God's sake, Bridget, what do you think I'm made of? If a girl is – like Bobby, and seems to – want a man's company, then only a very odd man would refuse what she puts on a plate for him! And I'm – a very normal sort of man. I take my pleasures where I can. But pleasure is one thing – and – and feeling is another. That's what I'm trying to tell you. I've – oh, for Christ's sake girl, I'm beginning to feel a great deal for you, and it's that that matters to me! I wanted you here this weekend to – to see if there could be a chance to talk to you properly. Whenever I've tried to get anywhere near you at the hospital, you've sheered away, slipped out of my fingers! Here, being down here for three days, I thought I'd stand a better chance of – of getting to know you. So now you know. And I'm damned if I'll apologise because I've been sleeping with Bobby – and I don't deny I have. She's – '

'I don't want to know – I don't want to know,' she cried, and then pulling blindly at the door, she ran out into the cold of the December night, running as fast as she could. Anywhere – she didn't care where to. Just to get away from the sound of his voice, the implications of what he had been saying.

Chapter 10

It was odd, somehow, the way everything about the Royal seemed to change, now that Bridget was no longer one of the four. It was the same hospital, the work was the same, the same people worked in it, but now, everything was different. She would come off duty alone, go to her room alone, spend her free time alone. The other nurses in her year all had their own friends, had had for a year or more, had made lives for themselves that included their friends, and there just wasn't any room for Bridget.

The strangest thing was the way Bobby and Judith would pass her in the corridors, or in the dining room, without a word, not appearing even to see her. It wasn't that they set out consciously to 'send her to Coventry'. It was simply that they had no further use for her, and as such, she just didn't exist. Liz would speak to her, however, when they did happen to meet, though even she seemed unwilling to do more than exchange casual greetings. Bridget knew that this was partly because of Bobby and Judith. She accepted that Liz felt a loyalty towards them, even while she did not really share their view of the world. And it was partly because of her ever-growing preoccupation with Ken. They were to be married as soon as Liz finished her training, and this was general knowledge among the nurses.

Bridget didn't mind her solitariness nearly as much as she had feared she would. Many times she would marvel at the old Bridget she had been, so frightened of loneliness, and would smile in her new-found maturity when she remembered how she had been at first. For Bridget had undoubtedly changed a good deal. The affair at Bobby's home at Christmas, as well as the episode on the ward with David before that, had pulled her up sharp, as it were, made her aware of herself and her responsibilities as she had never been before. The Sisters with whom she worked now told each other that that Nurse Preston was a different girl – that training had decidedly knocked the corners off, that the silent, still face of the old days had given way to a warmth, a friendliness. She was still reserved, but much of the diffidence of the old days, a diffidence that had looked like dumb insolence, had gone, as she developed both as a nurse and as a person. For she loved her work more and more, taking intense pleasure in every aspect of it. To her own surprise, she had a very real vocation for it – which, as she told herself wryly, was fortunate, seeing I took up nursing for any reason but that!

She saw little of the men, either. David, much to her relief, left the Royal shortly after Christmas, as his appointment was over and he was not offered a new one. Bridget wondered vaguely if the fact that he had come drunk to a ward had actually reached the ears of the senior medical staff, and whether this had anything to do with his not being reappointed, but dismissed the thought. She just wasn't interested, and that was that. David Nestor was a thing of the past, to be as forgotten as thoroughly as nursery school experiences.

Sometimes, she would see Josh crossing the court-yard, meet him in a corridor, or see him in the coffee shop, but she would merely nod, and hurry on when this happened. Once or twice he tried to stop her, to speak to her, but she would pull away, say she was in a hurry, and couldn't stop. She didn't know whether he was still going about with Bobby – and as the only gossip she ever heard was the general gossip that occupied the nurses in the dining-room or in the sitting-room at night, she had no way of finding out. She certainly didn't intend to ask.

She pushed the memory of what he had said that night at the house in Surrey firmly to the back of her mind. He had said enough to make her realise that he did, in fact, care a little for her, that it hadn't been the pity she abhorred that had prompted his kindness to her back in her early days at the Royal. And though she knew that she loved Josh Simpson very much indeed, that part of her always would, she had decided to cut her losses. It was impossible to follow up what he had said that night, impossible to allow her feelings for him to sway her. What was past was past. She had only one idea now; to finish her training, and then to leave the Royal for ever, and start a whole new life for herself somewhere abroad.

And then, half-way through her second year, she was sent to work in the operating theatres. She was alarmed at first, memories of her trips to that august department as a ward nurse stirring in her, but then she told herself sensibly that everyone who went there was new; they all had to learn, and she would learn too. And learn she did. Her days were a rush of sterilising, of running about as 'dirty nurse' for small cases, then larger and more complex cases, and the interminable cleaning that was so much a part of the work. And then, after her second month in the department, Theatre Sister sent for her.

'Now, Nurse Preston,' she said briskly. 'You've been on this department for eight weeks, hmm?'

'Yes, Sister.' Bridget felt a momentary sinking as she wondered whether she had done something wrong. It was not often Theatre Sister found time to call individual nurses to her office like this.

But Theatre Sister went on cheerfully, 'You seem to have an aptitude for this work – I've been watching you, and you're quick and deft – which a theatre nurse needs to be. Now, Nurse Jessolo is off sick – which means that the second theatre needs a new senior. Do you feel capable of coping with such work?'

Bridget gulped. The second theatre was the one which handled the smaller lists, the straightforward work like appendicectomies, herniorrhaphies, varicose vein ties, and the senior nurse there was the one who 'took table', who scrubbed up with the surgeons, handed instruments, and generally acted as the boss of the small theatre, under Sister's supervision.

'I – I think so, Sister,' she said. 'I'd certainly like to try.'

'Good,' Sister said briskly. 'Now, this is a good time for you to start – we're not too busy at present, and I've time to really teach you – the first list today is a small one – an appendix, excision of lipoma, and a hernia. You will scrub for it and I will act as your dirty nurse – so I'll be there to help if you get stuck. Come along now, and we'll get your instruments out, and check the layout.'

Bridget enjoyed that morning thoroughly. It felt odd at first to scrub up, to put on the sterile gown, to stand still while Sister tied the tapes, to put on the smooth, brown rubber gloves, but after the first few moments of strangeness, she forgot herself, and became absorbed in the operation. She found she knew more than she had realised that she knew. Almost without being told, she handed the surgeon – one of the younger consultants – the sponge forceps for the preliminary swabbing of the skin, spread the sterile towels over the area, clipped them into place, and swung smoothly into the routine of the operation.

When the last stitch was tied, and she took off the towels to fasten the dressing in position, the surgeon grinned at her cheerfully above his mask.

'First case, Nurse?' he said, as he stripped off his

118

gloves and dropped them into the bowl of saline beside him.

'Yes, sir,' Bridget said, looking at him sideways for signs of annoyance.

But he grinned even more, his eyes crinkling above the white line of his mask. 'Well done, then. To the manner born, eh, Sister?' And Sister, busily changing trolleys round, ready for the next case smiled too, and nodded. 'A credit to me, sir!' she said, they both smiled at Bridget in a way that made her glow with pride.

Within a week, Bridget was in full control of her new job. She found the work difficult enough to extend her fully, which was enjoyable, but not so difficult that she could not cope with any aspect of it. Sister, realising this, put more and more complicated operations on to the second theatre's lists, and by the end of a month Bridget felt herself to be the complete theatre nurse.

One of the best things about working in the second theatre was that Bridget hardly ever saw Josh at all. In the first eight weeks on the department, when she had been 'dirty nurse' in the main theatre, she had seen him almost every day, for he worked there constantly. But although there had been no occasion for them to talk to each other, except on purely professional matters, his presence had been distressing to her. Every time she had caught sight of his square shoulders, the muscles moving sleekly under the white gown as he worked, she felt her heart lurch, the painfully familiar sense of sheer physical excitement that he could arouse in her.

Sometimes she had caught his eyes as she moved about the theatre, when he looked up momentarily from his work to ask for something, once or twice he had turned his head towards her so that she could mop his forehead, as he sweated slightly under the hot, shadowless light, and these moments had been electric for her. It would take a long time for her to get over the way she felt about this man, she knew that, and seeing him so closely and so often only exacerbated her feelings. So it was an intense relief that she no longer had to see him, tucked away as she was in her own little second theatre.

And then, late one evening, just as she was going off duty, Theatre Sister called her from her office.

'Look, Preston, can you help me out tonight? There's a bit of a panic on in the private wing theatres – Sister there has flu, and her staff nurse has a septic finger, blast her, and can't scrub. So I've got to cover for them tonight. And Night Sister is off duty, and her deputy can't take any theatre cases if any emergencies come in, because she just isn't a theatre nurse. So that means I've got to put a middle-year nurse on call here tonight – what with Staff Nurse Casey being on holiday this week. Do you think you can manage that? The chances are nothing'll come in, of course – but it could happen, and if it does, someone from the department will have to be on call. Do you feel able?'

'I think so, Sister,' Bridget said slowly. 'I've scrubbed for most of the sorts of emergencies we get, haven't I? And if I get really stuck with something, I could get the junior to phone you in the wing to give advice?'

'Of course you could – and I'll probably be there all night God help me. They've got five labouring women in Private Maternity, and Sister there has warned me it's odds on two of them will need Caesars – *two* of them! Honestly, it never rains but it pours – '

'I hope I don't get a Caesar over here.' Bridget was alarmed. 'That's one thing I've never taken – '

'No, you should be all right there. General Maternity is full, and any new cases will have to go somewhere else on the Emergency Bed Service, and none of their people are likely to come here for anything. I've checked – the most they anticipate are a couple of high forceps, and they cope with those themselves – look, I'll have to go. They've still got a list going over in

120

Private Theatre and none of their people have had any off duty today, they're so short-staffed – I'll tell Night Sister you're on call – and here's hoping nothing comes in for you – 'Night, Preston. All the best!'

Bridget checked that all was clear in the theatres before taking herself off duty, also praying that nothing would come in. She was tired already – it had been a long day, and much as she enjoyed her work, she did not relish the idea of being dragged from a warm bed in the middle of the night to take another case.

She checked the list of surgeons on call before leaving the hospital for the Nurses' Home, and at what she saw there, prayed even harder that nothing would come in for theatre, for Josh was on call for main theatres that night, too.

But at the back of her mind, she knew something would come in. It was almost inevitable – her first time on call, and Josh on call too. And she was right.

At half past two, the night staff nurse came and shook her briskly, pulling her out of a confused dream about taking a Caesar all on her own, to tell her of a case that needed urgent surgery.

'I'm not sure what it's all about, Preston,' the night staff nurse said. 'It's all a bit hush-hush. All I know is it's a member of the staff, and whoever she is, she needs a laparotomy. I can't imagine *why* there's such a fuss, but there it is. They want the theatre ready for a laparotomy in half an hour, anyway. And Mr Simpson said to be ready for a pretty major job. He told me to tell whoever was on call to put out practically everything she could think of. I've put the sterilisers on for you – so jump about a bit!'

Bridget dressed with chilled fingers, her heart trembling within her. Of all things that could have come in, a laparotomy was the most terrifying. The patient needed an exploratory operation – and once the incision was made, and the condition explored, almost any operation might be needed. There was just no way of knowing what. She would indeed have to put out practically every instrument there was.

By the time she had arrived at the theatres, the junior on night duty had laid up almost completely, which was one comfort. Bridget had merely to select her instruments, get them boiling, and lay her trolley. She checked the theatre carefully for details before scrubbing up herself, and as a precaution, told the junior to prepare a small trolley for an intravenous infusion.

'This could be anything,' she told the scurrying junior, over her shoulder, as she scrubbed her hands and arms at the big white sink. 'And it's odds on the patient'll need some sort of IV – saline and glucose almost certainly, possibly blood. When you've done the trolley, ring the lab and see if any blood has been crossmatched for her, whoever she is.'

'Will they know, if I can't give them a name?' the junior asked, busily slapping bowls and instruments on to a small trolley.

'Probably,' Bridget said. 'They'll know who the emergency is, anyway. Unless there's another case for the Private Theatre – anyway, ask them.'

'Someone told me it's one of the nurses,' the junior said chattily. 'But I can't find out who – Night Sister was flying around like a flea in a fit, and no one dared ask her – you know what she's like when she's in a flap.'

Bridget laughed, and began to dry her hands on the sterile towel that lay ready for her. 'I do! But there usually is a fuss when it's staff that gets sick, you know that. We'll know who it is soon enough. Probably turn out to be an appendix, anyway – ' and under her breath, she muttered, 'I hope – '

She shrugged into her gown, and said without turning, 'Do up my tapes, Nurse, will you, before you make that phone call?'

But as she spoke, the big door of the sterilising room shushed open, and footsteps came purposefully across the floor.

Josh's voice made Bridget stiffen. 'I'll do it, Nurse. You go and make your phone call, whatever it is – '

Bridget felt his hands behind her as he took the tapes of her gown and began to tie them.

'I didn't know you were on call,' he said, and his voice was so low she could barely hear it above the hiss of the sterilisers.

'There was a shortage of staff over in the Private Theatres,' Bridget said evenly. 'So I had to cover here while Sister covers them. I can cope.'

'I'm sure you can.' He stood still watching her while she pulled on her gloves, and when she had finished, and turned to go into the theatre to arrange her instruments on the trolley, he said in a strained voice, 'Wait a minute. I – I want to talk to you about this case.'

Obediently she stopped, and picked up a sterile towel to wrap her gloved hands in, to keep them sterile while she waited for him to speak.

He stood undecided, his mask dangling below his chin, a white cap covering all but a rim of hair above his creased brow.

'Do you know who this patient is?' he asked abruptly, after a pause.

'No – only that it's a member of the staff. What's all the fuss about? I gather there *is* a bit of fuss going on.'

He nodded, then dropped his eyes. 'It's Bobby,' he said flatly.

Bridget felt sick for a moment. Not just because the patient they were preparing for was Bobby, but because of his obvious distress. Even though she knew that she had no hope – or even intention – of ever becoming any sort of friend, or more, of this man's, it hurt to discover that he still seemed to care something for

Bobby, despite what he had said about his feelings for her that night last Christmas.

'I see,' she said, after a moment. 'What's the matter? Is – is she very ill?'

'Very ill indeed,' he said, and then looked up at her, his eyes shadowed so that she couldn't see the expression in them. 'And you might as well know now as later. She – she's been very stupid – ' He swallowed. 'She was pregnant. And – and she's procured an abortion. I don't know the details, but I suppose she went to some botcher in a back street somewhere. Anyway, she's in a pretty bad state. God knows what we'll find when we open her up – '

Bridget stared at him, her thoughts swirling. Bobby, pregnant? An abortion?

He turned away, and with a vicious gesture, pulled his mask over his face and started to scrub his own hands.

'I know what you're thinking,' he said above the swish of the water. 'But – '

The big doors moved, and the junior came scurrying across the terrazzo floor.

'I say, Nurse Preston,' she gasped, heavy with her important news. 'I say, there *is* some blood crossmatched, and do you know who the patient is? It's Nurse Aston, and – '

'I know,' Bridget said heavily. 'I know. Get my instruments out of the steriliser, please, Nurse. We're in a hurry.'

As she sorted out haemostats and clamps, sponge forceps and needleholders, laying them in neat rows on the trolley, as she broke tubes of cat-gut, and laid the hanks of smooth, brown ties ready on a swab, she felt strangely numb. Part of her was distressed to think of Bobby being so ill – angry and hurt though she was whenever she thought of Bobby, badly as she felt Bobby had treated her, still, they had been friends, of a sort. And to think of the gay, noisy

124

Bobby as anything but bubbling with good health was sad.

But what hurt most was the way Josh had behaved when he told her the news. It seemed obvious to Bridget that the pregnancy Bobby had tried so disastrously to terminate was due to Josh. Why else should Josh seem so upset? But was he distressed because of the pregnancy, or because he had known – had allowed – Bobby to procure that abortion?

She remembered his voice as he said, ' – I don't know the details, but I suppose she went to some botcher in a back street somewhere – ' Was he telling the truth? Did he really not know? Or had he himself sent her to that botcher?

She tried not to think about it. One of the things about Josh that she had admired most was his approach to his work. He was gay, he joked with patients, he led a noisy and hectic life on as well as off duty – but somehow she had always been aware of his deep care for his work, his feelings about its importance. Had his relationship with Bobby so poisoned his attitudes that he had lost all ethical ideas? It was more than she could bear to think about.

And then, the big doors of the theatre swung open, and the trolley with its white-sheeted form trundled in, the porter at the foot, a weary anaesthetist guiding the head, while the junior pushed the big anaesthetic machine alongside. As the trolley came up to the table under the big, shadowless light, Josh came through from the sterilising room, and stood back to let the porter and junior nurse lift Bobby on to the table.

Bridget looked down at her, at the white face, crumpled and half hidden under the dark-green rubber of the anaesthetic mask, at the fair hair escaping from the white cap that was supposed to be covering it, at the rim of white showing under the half closed eyelids, and felt a wave of pity wash over her. To see the pretty, gay Bobby like this, helpless under her anaesthetic, her skin blotched red by the pressure of the anaesthetic mask, the half dried tears on the white skin of her cheeks, the tears that often accompanied unconsciousness, was agonising in its pathos.

'She's bloody low,' the anaesthetist grunted, lifting one eyelid with a practised finger to peer into the blank, blue eye beneath. 'She's in a high fever – and that doesn't help. I've given her a massive dose of penicillin, as an umbrella, but it's my guess you'll find a mass of infection there – she's been sitting on this for a week or more.'

'You managed to get some details?' Josh asked sharply, as he took the sponge forceps from Bridget, and began to swab the wide swathe of skin over the exposed abdomen with red mercurochrome.

'Yup.' The anaesthetist, a dour Scot, gave a quick snort of humourless laughter. 'I cheated. Gave her some of her pentothal, and then asked her a few questions before I put her right out. Christ, man, we had to find out *something*. She wouldn't tell us when she was first brought in, so what would you have me do? Maybe it's unethical, but she's too ill for me to give a good goddam about ethics.'

'So?' With a sign to Bridget, Josh began to spread the big towels in place, clipping them to expose just the square of the operation area.

'She was three months pregnant – her parents were away – on a tour or some such, and she was on holiday at home. So, she tried everything from quinine to gin to hot baths with no effect, and then went to some dirty old woman she heard of – God knows where from, but they always do hear somehow. She had a sort of operation eight days ago – and I gather she had no anaesthetic, poor little devil – and started to feel ill a day or so later. Seems a daily help her family employs came to

126

the house to get it ready for her parents' return, and found her collapsed in the bathroom – and had the sense to get in touch with a doctor. Who sent her back here. And that's about it – '

Josh stood very still for a moment, and then said, 'Well, at least we know. I couldn't find out anything. She wouldn't talk to me. All I could get out of her was that she – she had been pregnant and now she wasn't.' He took a deep breath, and then thrust a hand at Bridget. 'Can we start, McPherson?'

'She's as fit as she'll ever be,' the anaesthetist said. 'And the quicker you start the sooner you'll finish – so get on with it, man.'

With cold fingers, Bridget put a gleaming scalpel into Josh's hand, and watched, her face rigid under her mask as he made the first sweeping incision, from umbilicus to pubis. As the orange-painted skin parted, and the first small blood vessels spurted vividly, she found her head swimming. She had seen this many times before, but this was Bobby, Bobby – and then, as though from a distance she heard Josh snap, 'Spencer Wells – Nurse, Spencers – ' and she pulled herself together, and slapped a pair of forceps into his hand, so that he could clip the vessels.

Soon, the wound sprouted a twinkling fringe of forceps, and with deft fingers Josh tied each bleeding point and discarded the used forceps for the junior to collect and reboil for later use. Bridget, her hands moving automatically, helped, swabbing, handing instruments and ties, acting as assistant surgeon, because there was no other doctor available at this hour to assist in her stead.

She felt like an actor in a weird film, one of a group of white-gowned, head-bent people, encapsulated in the glare of the big light, while a soft-footed nurse padded busily about in the shadows beyond the focus of the table, helping the anaesthetist set up a blood transfusion. Her hands and Josh's, so similar in characterless brownness, moved easily and smoothly about their work.

Then, Josh straightened, and grunted softly, angrily:

'The uterus is perforated – and she's full of pus. You were right about that, McPherson. I – I don't think I can suture it – it's a huge tear – and both tubes are heavily infected – '

There was an agonising silence. 'Well, man, you've got a consent form signed, haven't you? The girl's over twenty-one – just. She was fit to sign it – so you'd better do what you've got to do,' McPherson said heavily.

'Twenty-one – ' Josh said. 'Christ, I can't – '

The anaesthetist leaned forwards and said grimly, 'I know how you'll be feeling, but use your head, man, not your sentiments. Even if you do suture her, what'll happen? At best, you'll get a uterus so scarred she'll have no hope in hell of ever conceiving again – and with both tubes as far gone as those are, even if her uterus *is* salvaged, will she ever manage another baby? I doubt it. And at worst, suture it, close her up, and with all the antibiotics in the world, it's likely the thing'll break down, and she'll have to come to theatre again to have a hysterectomy then – use your head, man – '

Josh raised his head and looked miserably at the anaesthetist. The theatre was absolutely silent except for the faint hiss of gas from the anaesthetic machine. Slowly, Josh turned his head and looked at Bridget, and she felt her throat constrict at the agony in his eyes.

Then he said thickly, 'You're right – but it's a hell of a thing to have to do – '

'Ay, it is,' the anaesthetist said briskly. 'One hell of a thing. But she'll hardly survive at all if you don't, and you know it – '

Josh nodded, and with a glance at Bridget, said grimly, 'Right. Hysterectomy it is. Uterus and tubes

– though I think it'll be safe to leave the ovaries – they seem healthy enough, thank God – Nurse – '

And Bridget handed him a big retractor, and watched him make the first steps towards ensuring that never again would Bobby have a pregnancy, wanted or unwanted. And she felt tears slide down her face as the operation went on, to sting her cheeks with pain for Bobby.

Chapter 11

The hospital seethed with gossip, knots of nurses standing chattering in corners in the courtyard, scattering guiltily when Sisters went by, only to reassemble like flocks of starlings when they had gone. Despite the attempts of the administrative staff to keep the facts quiet, everyone knew that Bobby Aston had nearly died, and exactly why, and they all knew, too, that she had had a hysterectomy, and it was this that made them talk in frightened awe, yet with the sort of relish that such gossip always engenders.

Matron, deeply distressed, not only because of what had happened but because she felt she had had so little insight that she had been unable to see that Bobby was a girl to whom such a thing *could* happen, managed to derive some small comfort from this.

'Perhaps it's as well they do know,' she told Sister Chessman as they sat one morning over coffee, discussing the whole business. 'I'd have preferred to have kept it quiet, if only for Nurse Aston's sake – but perhaps it'll have a deterrent effect, I mean, the fact that the poor child had a hysterectomy. I don't believe in trying to keep young girls on the straight and narrow by using fear, by warning them of the "horrid consequences" when they do go wrong, but there's no doubt this has stopped a few of them in their tracks.'

Sister Chessman nodded. 'Mmm. I've been listening to them chatter – and there's not one that doesn't see what an awful thing it is to lose all hope of having children of your own when you're only twenty-one. What's happening to Aston?'

Matron sighed, and lit a cigarette. 'I've seen the parents – and a right pair they are! You can see why Aston's the sort of person she is. No regret about it – not a bit. No feeling on their part that they let her down, that they just didn't take enough interest in her – just annoyed it's happened – it gets in the way of their private plans, I gather. They'll have to take her off to convalescence somewhere now – and it was much simpler to have her safely tucked up here – so they thought. My God, some of these parents!'

'Any idea who – who the father was?' Sister Chessman asked curiously.

'I haven't asked her,' Matron said. 'It's happened, and if she doesn't want to tell me off her own bat, I can't pry.'

'I'm wondering if it's Mr Simpson, frankly.'

'Who can say? I know they did go about together a good deal – but according to the ward Sisters, they haven't been seeing as much of each other as they once did.'

Sister Chessman laughed shortly. 'They should know. Honestly, the gossip that goes on in the Sisters' sitting-room – '

Matron smiled grimly. 'I know, I know. And perhaps I shouldn't listen to as much as gets to me – but if I didn't I'd know all too little about what goes on – and I feel I should – '

Bridget, intensely unhappy, moved through the days, working automatically, sick with reaction whenever she thought of Josh and Bobby. She assumed, reasonably enough, that the relationship had gone on as before, that Josh and Bobby were still enjoying their full-blown affair, and that inevitably, Josh had been the father of the child Bobby didn't want – so desperately didn't want.

She managed to understand, much as it hurt her to think of it, why the affair existed. Bobby was 'available' and as Josh had said to her that night, it would be an odd man who did not take advantage of the fact. She found it impossible to realise, however, that such an affair could exist in the absence of love on Josh's part. Bridget, still very inexperienced in the ways of men, took it for granted that a man functioned as she did – that he could only sleep with a girl he loved – for she was an intensely feminine person, and knew instinctively that for her, at any rate, such love-making and real love were indivisible. One could not exist without the other.

So she went about her work in a state of numb misery. However much she told herself that there was no possible chance of her ever being able to think of Josh and herself as a unit, which in her heart of hearts she knew she wanted more than anything else in the world, she still could not help feeling bereft when she thought of his love for Bobby – which she was convinced he felt.

And yet, she would tell herself, sick at heart, and yet, he let her do this dreadful thing to herself, despite the fact he was a doctor, despite the fact that he loved her. How could he? How could he? she would ask herself with dreary insistence. How could he?

So, when Josh came to the second theatre late one evening, to talk to her, she made every effort she could not to respond to him.

He came and stood at the door, barring her from leaving and she stood rigid on the far side of the narrow operating table and looked at him, at the unwontedly unsmiling expression on his face, and said desperately, 'Please, go away. I don't want to talk to you – I just don't want to talk to you.'

He shook his head at that. 'But you're going to – *you are going to*. There – there are things I've got to tell you, and I must tell you. For God's sake, Bridget, be fair. I care about you – do you understand? I've *got* to talk to you – '

But she blazed at him, her cheeks showing high spots of colour, her eyes sparkling with anger, an anger that was the only thing that prevented her from crying out, from throwing herself into his arms, from telling him that she loved him, and didn't care about anything else – she loved him –

But she used her anger to push her feelings down, and said between clenched teeth. 'I *won't* talk to you – I won't – after what has happened – after Bobby – No!' and she crossed the theatre, to push him forcibly away, so that he had been unable to keep her there.

She wondered for a while whether the best thing for her to do would be to leave the Royal altogether. Somehow, it was all such a mess. She would sit in her room, alone, staring out of the window into the garden, thinking till her head swam.

Liz came to her there, one afternoon, while she was sitting with a textbook in front of her, making a poor pretence at studying, and stood diffidently at the door, hovering anxiously as she looked at Bridget sitting still by her window.

'Can – can I come and talk to you?' she said, her face a little flushed. 'I – I've got a message for you.'

Bridget stood up awkwardly. It had been so long since there had been any real contact between Liz and herself that she felt almost as awkward and strange as she had on that very first morning in the Preliminary Training School, so long ago now.

'Of course – of course,' she said. 'Er – shall I make a cup of tea? I wasn't going to go to tea in the dining-room – and I'm due back on duty at five – ' She was talking just to make conversation now, as she looked covertly at Liz's strained face.

'Er – er – no thanks. I'm not really thirsty – ' Liz came across the room to perch uncomfortably on the edge of the bed, and began to twist her fingers in her lap.

'Look, Bridget – ' she began. Then stopped.

'Well?'

Liz took a deep breath. 'I've got a message for you – from Bobby.'

Bridget stiffened. 'Oh?' she said politely, her face smooth, not wanting to let Liz see how she felt about Bobby.

Liz leaned forward impulsively. 'Oh, Bridget, please – don't be angry. She knows she treated you badly – but she's truly sorry – I think – and she wants to talk to you. She – she needs a friend, you know. Very much.'

Bridget raised her eyebrows at that. 'Oh, come off it, Liz. She doesn't need *me*. What about you – and Judith?'

'Judith!' Liz put a world of scorn into the name. 'Judith makes me *sick*. She won't go near Bobby. Scared Matron'll think she's the same sort of person Bobby is, and terrified the old girl'll tell her parents – and you know what her father's like. Not that that's any excuse. Because Judith *is* like Bobby. I mean, Judith – well, she's been behaving just as Bobby did. The only difference is, she's been lucky, and got away with it. It's Bobby who – got caught.'

'Hasn't she even been to see Bobby in the sick bay?'

'Not her! I tell you, Judith has dropped Bobby as though she never even met her! She's going around the place as though butter wouldn't melt in her mouth, too bloody good to be true. And you can bet your bottom dollar she'll go on that way. No, Bobby's got no friend in Judith.'

'What about you, then?' Bridget said evenly. 'Or are you scared to admit that you're a friend of Bobby's, too?'

Liz flushed. 'No! It's not like that at all! I – I haven't

been as close to the others as I was before – before last Christmas, I mean. Ken – well, he and me – we were both so sick about what happened – I mean, we had no idea that you didn't care for David Nestor. We thought you did – and that – oh, I don't know. It's funny, really. When – when you're really in love with someone, you think every other couple is the same as you are. Ken and me, we both thought that you and David, and Bobby and Josh, and Judith and Clive were like us. In love, you see, and – and only wanting to be – together *because* you were in love. And when we realised that you – that Bobby had sort of engineered you into coming down that weekend, that you didn't even know what she was up to, we felt sick. And since then, I just haven't been so friendly. I mean – I didn't *drop* them or anything – I'm not like that. I just haven't been so friendly.'

'And now, you don't want to see Bobby at all,' Bridget said flatly.

'Oh, let me finish, Bridie, please!' Liz said urgently. 'It's not that at all. Look, Ken has a new job – he goes to Scotland next month to a junior consultancy – it's marvellous, really. I mean, we'll be able to get married almost right away. And I've asked Matron to arrange for me to finish my training at the same hospital where Ken will be. They don't mind married students there, Matron says, and she'll – give me a good reference. So I won't be here, you see. So, like I said, Bobby – needs a friend.'

Bridget stood up, and began to prowl restlessly about the room. 'Look, Liz. I know you mean well – but how can I just – just go and see Bobby as though nothing ever happened? I – I thought you three were such wonderful people – especially Bobby. You were everything I ever wanted to be – gay and relaxed and happy – you know? And I needed you all as friends so much. That was – why it all happened, really. I was so scared you'd not want me if I didn't go along with you – with Bobby, really, though I thought you were all the same, I suppose. And then – then you – she let me down. It hurt. A lot. I've – got used to being on my own again, like I always was. It doesn't matter so much any more. I don't think I could bear to start again. Not after what's happened.' She stopped by Liz, then, and said earnestly, 'Please, don't think – that it's a *moral* thing. That I – don't approve of what Bobby did. I mean, I *don't* – I think it's – awful. Sickening. But I'm not the sort to turn my back on someone just because I think they've been stupid, and behaved badly. It's just that I don't think I *could* be a friend of hers again.'

'Poor Bridget,' Liz said softly. 'I just didn't know. That you were so – lonely. I thought you were reserved because you *liked* to be that way. You were – sweet and quiet, and I left it at that. I never thought very much about what went on behind people's faces – not till I met Ken and – fell in love with him. I've grown up a bit since then. I'm sorry about it all, really I am, Bridie. If – if I'd *known* what Bobby was like, what she would do to you, I'd never have just sat by. But I didn't know, truly I didn't.'

'I believe you,' Bridget said.

Liz smiled crookedly at that. 'Well, that's something. But about Bobby, Bridget. I see what you mean – but couldn't you at least go and see her? She wants you to – and the least you could do is to tell her yourself how you feel.'

There was a long pause, then Bridget said unwillingly, 'All right. I'll go and see her. But only to make it clear that I can't just pick up again where I left off.' Impulsively, she leaned over, and hugged Liz warmly.

'And I'm awfully pleased about you and Ken, Liz, truly I am. I hope you'll both be very happy, and – and have a marvellous life together up in your Scottish hospital.'

Liz lit up at the thought of her bright future.

'Isn't it marvellous? I'm so lucky, Bridget, and I know it. Ken's a wonderful person – '

She glowed as she thought of her Ken, then looked shrewdly at Bridget. 'What about you, Bridie? I know now that you never cared for David, but isn't there anyone else on the horizon for you? It's so lovely to be in love – I sort of want to see everyone else as happy as I am.'

'Me?' Bridget managed a smile. 'Oh, don't think about me! I'm not the marrying sort, I suppose. I mean, when you all used to talk about meeting doctors here, and marrying one, I never really saw it as you all did – '

Liz made a face. 'Don't remind me about the way we used to talk. I – don't think I meant it, really. I used to talk like the others did because it seemed the – smart thing to do. I didn't set out to – to catch Ken, honestly I didn't. It just happened.'

Bridget laughed then. 'I believe you,' she said again, and Liz, too, laughed, and relaxed a little.

They talked of casual things then, and when it was time for them both to go back on duty, they walked across the courtyard in companionable silence. At the door to the main block, where they parted, Bridget to return to Theatre, Liz to go back to the Gynae ward she was now working on, Liz said impulsively, 'I'm sorry I'm going away, in one way. I mean, you and I could be real friends I think. Will you write to me?'

'I will,' Bridget promised, and smiled. 'And knit things for your babies too.'

Liz laughed. 'Plenty of time for that,' she said. 'But I hope I have dozens some day.' She sobered then. 'Poor Bobby – '

'Yes – ' Bridget said. 'I suppose so. Poor Bobby – '

There were no cases that evening on Theatre, only a mass of clearing up from the day's lists, and Bridget settled to the long tedious chores with a sigh. She had promised Liz she would go and see Bobby, and she would keep her promise. But she didn't relish the idea of facing her one bit.

'I'll go tonight, after I get off duty,' she told herself, as she industriously scrubbed instruments, and laid them in neat rows in the gleaming cupboards. 'Better get it over with – '

When she went up to supper, an hour before she was due off duty, she stopped at the porter's lodge in the main hall to see if there were any letters. The only letters she ever got were the monthly, short, typewritten notes from Mr Lessiter, who wrote out of a sense of duty about his guardianship, notes which Bridget as dutifully answered. One of these letters was due, so Bridget thought she might as well go and see if it had arrived.

It had, and she took it from the porter with a brief thanks, and turned to go, tucking it into her apron bib.

But he called her back. 'Nurse Preston! There's something else for you – ' He leered at her. 'By hand, this one – ' and he gave her a thick white envelope, with her name written across it in a firm hand.

She stared at the envelope, and said wonderingly. 'For me?'

'You're the only Preston we've got, ducks!' the porter said. 'It's for you, all right – '

She tucked it into her apron with the other letter, and went on to supper with a faint frown on her face. Though she had no idea who the letter was from, not recognising the handwriting, she felt obscurely that this was something to be read in privacy, that it was somehow too important to read in public. So she hurried through her meal, and went back to the peace of the quiet theatres to perch on a tall stool in the sluice, out of Sister's way, to slit the envelope in peace.

'My dear Bridget,' she read. 'Since you flatly refuse to

139

talk to me, this is about the only way I can communicate with you. For God's sake, Tiddler, *read* this. Don't just screw it up. That would be childish, wouldn't it? And I don't think you are as petty as that, even if you do refuse to talk to me.

'In a way, it's easier to write all this than to say it. When you stand and stare at me with those big, grey eyes of yours, all icy, I find myself almost at a loss for words – which is an extraordinary way for *me* to be. But that is the effect you have on me – if you didn't, believe me, you wouldn't be able to get away from me as you always do.

'Tiddler, dear Tiddler. I've been trying to tell you for a long time that I care a great deal for you – I've watched you this past year or more, watched you with David, and since, on your own, and I have ached to know you better. There is something about you that makes me – I don't know. I've certainly never felt about any other girl as I do about you. And that brings me to what I must say to you.

'From the beginning, I've spent a lot of time with Bobby. I don't for a moment intend to pretend otherwise. But I want you to know that she meant no more to me than any other girl has ever meant – someone who was – fun, if you like. You must try to understand, Tiddler. Ever since I was little more than a kid, I've liked girls. And they've liked me. Does that sound big-headed? I suppose it does. But there it is. I've slept around – my God, but that looks revolting in cold print! But it's true. If a girl was willing, then I was too. But if you can understand this, it never meant anything to me more than a passing affair. Fun. Immoral, I suppose – but I've no great claims to being a great moralist. I've seen sex as – as an appetite like any other, one to be satisfied where and when I could.

'But now, I feel very different. I don't want any more of these grubby affairs. For the first time in

140

my life, I'm in love. And now I've said it. I'm in love, with you, my own Tiddler, and somehow, I've got to make you see that, got to make you see me, if you possibly can, with new eyes. Try to forget that I was the man you knew, who carried on an affair with a friend of yours. Can you forgive that? Can you try to see me as a man who loves you very much indeed, and wants nothing more than to spend the rest of his life with you?

'And to make sure the slate is clean, to help me more than you really, there's something else I want you to know. This grim business about Bobby. I had no part in it – to put it bluntly, her pregnancy was not due to me. I *know* that. That night at Bobby's place last Christmas finished things as far as I was concerned. I can still see your face that night, and I feel sick with anger whenever I remember it. You must believe this, Tiddler, you must.

'Please, my own love, please, think about this. And talk to me about it. I love you. And even if you feel now that you can't forgive me, please give me a chance. *Talk* to me. Let's spend some time together. Give yourself a chance to get to know me. Then, if you can't love me, I'll try to accept the fact with the best grace I can muster. But somehow, I'm going to *make* you care for me as I care for you. I *must*. You're the most wonderful thing that has ever happened to me. Josh.'

She sat for a long time, after she had folded the letter and put it back into her apron bib. A long time, not thinking, just sitting staring at the tiled wall of the sluice.

Then, she took a deep, shuddering breath, and dropping her head into her hands, wept bitterly. It was almost more than she could bear. That Josh should write as he had, that he loved her – nothing else mattered. The past, his and Bobby's, was

141

dead, and a bright, a glittering future stretched ahead of her. And she wept as though her heart would break, her mind whirling with the pain and the joy of it all.

Chapter 12

She went off duty at half past eight, leaving the theatres clean and quiet behind her, smiling so brilliantly in response to Theatre Sister's 'Goodnight' that the lady told herself in surprise that young Preston looked positively beautiful tonight. And then sighed sharply as she remembered the days when she, too, had been able to look like that.

Bridget stood undecided outside the big double doors for a moment. What she wanted to do was to go over to her room to re-read Josh's letter, now sitting warmly inside her apron, feeling as heavy as if it were written on a clay tablet. But she had promised to go and see Bobby. And somehow she felt obscurely that until she had seen Bobby, made the break with the past complete, as it were, she could not really think properly about what Josh had written.

So she straightened herself, took a deep breath, and walked purposefully along the corridor towards the doors that led to the little complex of private rooms that was the staff sick bay.

There was a staff nurse on duty there, sitting writing a report in her little office, and she nodded in response to Bridget's request to visit Nurse Aston.

'All right. She's much better – probably going convalescent in a week or so, and Matron said she could have visitors. Nip along – she's in the end room on the right.'

At the door, Bridget stood for a long moment,

then took another deep breath, and tapped on the panels.

'Come in,' Bobby's voice came muffled from the other side, and Bridget opened the door and went in, to close it behind her so that she could lean against it.

Bobby was sitting up in bed, the only light in the room coming from the bulb above her head, a light that cocooned her in brightness, lighting her fair hair to a gleaming sheet of blondeness.

When Bobby raised her head, Bridget gasped a little with shock. The beautiful round face, the sleek health that had always invested that face with a peach-like bloom, had gone. Her cheeks were thinner, her eyes so deeply shadowed in their sockets that they seemed to be violet in colour. Her temples were translucent, giving her face a mask-like look that aged her immeasurably.

There was a long silence, while the two girls stared at each other. Then Bobby said huskily, 'Hello, Bridget.'

'Hello, Bobby.' Bridget managed a narrow-lipped smile. 'How are you?'

Bobby stretched her arms above her head, letting the diaphanous sleeves of her blue nightdress fall back, so that Bridget could see that even her arms had become stick-like in their thinness. 'As well as can be expected. Isn't that what they always say?' Bobby said, and dropped her hands on to the covers again. 'It – it's nice of you to come, Bridie, love.'

Somehow, the familiar expression made Bridget want to cry. This girl was such a wreck of the old Bobby, so different, that to hear familiar words on her lips was eerie, somehow.

'Liz – said you wanted to see me,' she said baldly, sounding curt in her effort to control the rush of feeling Bobby's greeting had roused in her.

'Come and sit down, Bridie,' Bobby said. 'There's a chair over there.'

Obediently, Bridget brought the chair, and came and

144

sat beside the bed, folding her apron neatly on her lap for something to do – anything to avoid looking at Bobby.

'Bridie – I – I owe you an apology. I've owed it to you for a very long time. And I – wanted to tell you so.'

'Please – ' Bridget began. 'Please, Bobby, don't – '

'But I must,' Bobby said, almost fretfully. 'I must. I treated you badly, Bridie, and I know it. I shouldn't have – I shouldn't have let you think that weekend was going to be anything other than what it was – '

Bridget bit her lip. 'Well, I suppose I should have realised,' she said slowly. 'I – was a bit naive, to put it mildly.'

'Honestly, Bridie – I didn't know. I truly thought you *liked* David – I had no idea he'd turn so – nasty. If I had known – '

'Oh, Bobby, for God's sake!' Bridget was angry suddenly. 'Don't try and tell me that. I mean, if you really *were* surprised, as you suggest, when he – he got so nasty – you wouldn't have told Josh to – leave us alone. And you did. That's what hurt me most I think. I mean, David – David tried to – to – '

'To force you to sleep with him,' Bobby said, watching Bridget as she said it.

'Yes. And when Josh interfered, you told him to leave us alone – to let us sort it out for ourselves. And that – wasn't kind, to put it at it's mildest.'

'I know – I know.' Bobby began to pleat the sheet between her fingers. 'I – I didn't think.'

'And you told me I'd ruined the weekend, remember? Ruined the weekend! You didn't seem to care – care about what might have happened to me – '

'Please, Bridie, don't,' Bobby said. 'I'm truly sorry, really I am. Can't you forgive me? Can't we be friends again?'

Bridget looked at her, at the appealing expression in her shadowed eyes, and said abruptly, 'Tell me something, Bobby. Why did you ever want me to be one of – of your set? I mean, I wasn't a bit like you. I needed *you* all right – I know that. I was lonely, and awkward, and shy, and you three – specially you – you sort of dazzled me. But why did you want to include *me* in your life? I don't understand it. I was – dull. Naive. Always trying to back out of things. Yet you kept on at me – got mad when I tried to – to tell you I didn't like David, made me go on with him, because if I hadn't you'd have dropped me. That mattered to me – a lot. But why should it have mattered to you? I don't understand.'

Bobby shrugged slightly. 'I don't really know. I – just liked you, I suppose.'

With a sudden shrewdness, Bridget said, 'Was it because I helped you all with your work? Did your notes and all that?'

Bobby had the grace to blush slightly. 'A –little, perhaps. But it was more than that. I *did* like you – I still do – you were calm, and quiet, and I suppose I needed that.'

Bridget laughed shortly. 'You needed me for that? Not really. Bobby. Not really.'

Bobby looked at her sideways, through lowered lids, then with an apparent effort said. 'All right. I'll tell you. And you won't like it.'

'I'd like to know, all the same.'

Bobby let her head droop, so that her hair swung forwards and hid her face, while she watched her fingers at their incessant pleating of the sheet.

'It was Josh,' she said in a low voice. 'Josh.'

Bridget felt herself go cold suddenly.

'I knew – he liked you,' Bobby said. 'At that party – do you remember that first party in the mess? He – he looked at you. And I knew he liked you. And – I liked him. Very much. I – wanted him. And I knew enough to see that the only way I could make sure he'd – go

146

on seeing me for any length of time was if you were included in the things we did. If you were around. So – so I planned it so that you always were.'

Bridget stared at her, her heart sick. 'And you pushed me at David – '

'I pushed you at David so that Josh could see he was wasting his time yearning after you. It was easy then – he was attracted to you, I knew that, but not so much that he'd march off or anything if he saw you with someone else. I thought if he saw you with David, he'd give up, and settle for me.' She raised her head then, and looked at Bridget, her eyes glinting with something of the old Bobby. 'And he did, didn't he?'

'Yes,' Bridget said in a low voice. 'He did.'

'I suppose I've mucked it all up for you, Bridie, and I'm sorry.' Bobby's voice was smooth. 'If I hadn't been around, you and Josh – maybe you would have got somewhere with him. But I *was* – '

Bridget closed her eyes. To look at this girl, to hear her admitting that she had set out to take away from her the only man she had ever really cared about was dreadful. But the voice went on, inexorably.

'It's too late for you now, Bridie. Josh is mine now.'

Bridget opened her eyes then, and looked at her with a startled expression.

'Yours?'

'Of course.' Bobby smiled, sleekly. 'He's – an honourable type, old Josh. He – won't leave me in the cart now. Not after – what's happened to me.'

'What – what do you mean?' Bridget's own voice sounded cracked. 'What do you mean?'

Bobby opened her eyes widely at her, and smiled. 'Well, it's obvious, isn't it? I know I'm not having the baby – won't ever have a baby' – and at the sight of the sudden pain that crossed Bridget's face, she laughed aloud – 'no need to look like that – I'm not cut out for motherhood – it doesn't matter to me that I'll never be

147

saddled with brats – but even though I'm not having his baby, Josh isn't the type to leave me to dree my own weird, as they say – '

'His baby?' Bridget whispered. 'His?'

'Who else's?' Bobby put a pained expression on her face. 'My dear Bridie, who else's?'

'He – does he know?' Bridget said.

'Of course he does! Poor old Josh – he was sick when he realised I'd gone to that ghastly woman, and saw what she'd done to me, but he knows I did it for him. He doesn't want kids any more than I do – '

Somehow, Bridget got to her feet, somehow, managed to walk to the door.

'Don't go, Bridie – ' Bobby sat in her pool of light and looked across the room to where Bridget stood shaking and almost in tears.

'Can't we let bygones be bygones?' Bobby said sweetly. 'Can't we?'

Bridget shook her head. 'No – Bobby. No,' she said, almost in a whisper. 'Not now. Goodbye, Bobby,' and she pulled the door open, to almost fall out into the corridor.

And behind her, in the quiet room, Bobby snuggled deep into her pillows, her arms behind her head, and smiled up at the ceiling.

Bridget reached her room, the haven of her room, almost without knowing how she got there. And then sat in her chair by the window, staring out at the winking lights of the hospital, away over the garden, feeling as though she were so much dead flesh, not a person at all. He had lied to her. Lied to her. The words thumped and twisted in her head until she wanted to scream. He had lied to her. The happiness that had so short a time ago seemed so close within her grasp had gone, gone for always. There was nothing left.

She slept fitfully, tossing on her bed, sinking into vague and terrifying dreams that brought her sitting bolt upright, shaking, her eyes wet with tears. And so odd was the night, so confused her feelings, that when the night staff nurse suddenly appeared at her door, to switch the light on and fill the room with dazzle, she wasn't even surprised.

'Sorry to get you out, Preston,' Staff Nurse said. 'But there's an emergency call.'

Bridget blinked at her stupidly from her pillows. 'An emergency?'

'There's been a multiple smash-up on the motorway – four lorries and a motorbike and a couple of cars – a right holocaust. The police want an emergency medical team, and the ambulance depot can't help because their team is out on another call at a factory some place. Night Sister says they need two good surgical nurses – and the Casualty Department is full, so we can't send any of our people. And the theatres are working tonight on top of it. There's only you and Jessolo available, so you'll have to get up – Come on, girl – it's an emergency!'

Almost in a dream, she dressed, climbing into slacks and a sweater rather than uniform, for the staff nurse told her that this was the best clothing for what she would have to do, and followed the impatient older girl across the dark courtyard to the hospital.

There was a hospital ambulance waiting there, its engine ticking over, and as Bridget arrived, Nurse Jessolo appeared behind her, her eyes still thick with sleep, also in slacks and a sweater.

The ambulance driver leaned over, and hauled the two girls in beside him.

'Come on you two – the doctors are in the back – we'd better get moving – ' and as they huddled themselves into the small space beside him, the engine roared, and with a wide sweep of its headlights that threw the walls of the courtyard into glittering brilliance, the ambulance shot out of the hospital gates and on its way.

149

They sped through the silent streets, past shops with windows blank behind their blinds, along the shining tarmac, wet from the thick mist that lay close to the ground. As the ambulance reached the flyover that led on to the motorway, the fog seemed to thicken, to swirl in patches that made Bridget's eyes smart, and set Jessolo coughing.

They came on the scene of the smash-up almost with shock. One minute there was nothing but the patches of fog, the brilliance of the headlights on it, then there was noise, and light, and people.

One lorry lay on its side, two more piled drunkenly alongside it. Police, with huge emergency spotlights, and firemen, their black coats seeming to gleam yellowly in the light, were clambering over the wreckage, while alongside, on the grey-looking grass of the verge, three bodies lay under police greatcoats, ominously still.

The ambulance drew up alongside the lorries, its wheels screaming in protest at the sharp braking, and the girls tumbled out, Bridget bewildered and frightened at the noise, the suddenness of it all. At the back of the ambulance, the driver fumbled with the doors, and three men jumped out, to stand blinking in the light for a moment. Two of them, grabbing the bags of equipment the driver tossed out, made a beeline for the people lying on the verge and one, as he passed Bridget and Nurse Jessolo called out, 'Hey – you two –'

It was the senior RSO, and still in her dream-like state, Bridget, with Jessolo close behind, followed him and the other man towards the side of the road.

A policeman seemed to materialise from out of the fog and stopped them.

'Hospital? Thank God you got here – listen – two of them are dead, far as we can tell. T'other's pretty

150

rocky – out cold, and breathing bad. Chest stoved in, seemingly – '

The RSO nodded. 'Right – Prater' – he nodded at the other doctor with him – 'take one of the nurses and have a look – '

'And there's a car under the other side of that lorry,' the policeman went on. 'And there's someone in there moaning – woman – can't get much out of her but moans – and the other car's over there – and the motor-cyclist – got a kid under it. They're trying to get him and the driver out now – '

'Right – ' the RSO said crisply. 'I'll take that car. Simpson – you take the other nurse, and see about the woman – get on – ' and he ran across the road to disappear into the yellow mud of the fog.

For a moment, Bridget stood rigid, for the first time realising that the last of the three men who had been in the back of the ambulance was Josh. Then, as Dr Prater ran towards the men at the side of the road, with Nurse Jessolo loping awkwardly behind him, she felt his hand on her arm.

'Come on,' he said briefly. 'Work to be done – ' and she let him pull her along with him, to the far side of the crumpled lorries, her feet icy with cold, her body shaking with fear, in anticipation of what she might see.

The car was a little red mini, looking like a toy as it lay crushed under one huge wheel of the articulated lorry almost on to of it. The side nearest the driver was miraculously free, and Josh dropped to one knee beside the fireman who was beside it, working to free the jammed door with an acetylene blow-torch.

'Nearly got it,' the man grunted, his face lit to a ghastly blueness in the light of his torch. 'Nearly got it – '

She could hear the unearthly moaning that was coming from the car, above the noise of the torch,

151

above the sounds of shouting voices and engines that filled the night with hideous sound. A rhythmic even moaning that filled her with sick terror.

'Got it,' the fireman said, and the door swung back on its ruined hinges, to lean drunkenly against the bonnet.

Josh, his back straining, moved swiftly. Bridget could see his arms flex, the muscles strain hard, as he backed away from the car, a woman held awkwardly in his arms, her head thrown back against his arm, her mouth wide and red as she moaned and moaned interminably.

'Easy does it, girl, easy does it,' Josh was murmuring. 'We've got you, lovey, we've got you – easy does it now – ' He straightened, and moving with cat-like smoothness, carried her to the side of the road, to lay her down on the big tarpaulin a policeman had laid ready.

Bridget, following, dropped to her knees beside the tarpaulin, and as Josh felt for her pulse, and then started to straighten the bent legs, she leaned over the moaning woman, and murmured, gently, as though to a crying baby, 'It's all right, my dear, it's all right – we've got you – there's a doctor here, and we've got you – don't cry, we've got you – '

The woman opened terrified brown eyes, the whites showing all round the edge of the iris, and her moaning changed, became gasping.

'Baby – baby – baby,' she said, her voice rising to a scream at the end of it. Then she arched her neck, and opened her mouth wide to scream in agony once more.

Bridget looked up, to where Josh was kneeling beside her, pulling the woman's coat from her sides, and as she did so, his face whitened in the fitful light.

'Oh, my God, she's pregnant – ' He put a hand

152

on the distended abdomen, and leaned towards the woman's face.

'Listen, my love – listen – don't scream, try not to scream – tell me – how far on are you?'

She opened her eyes again, to stare at him in terror, and her lips pulled back over her teeth in a feline grimace.

'Eight – eight months – baby – eight months – ' she said, and again, arched her neck, and screamed.

Bridget, clutching at the woman's icy hands, held on to her like grim death, feeling utterly helpless, only able to offer her own physical presence as a help in the woman's agony.

Josh's voice came crisply, 'That's a contraction – and a strong one – she's gone into labour – how long was she under that lorry?' and the policeman's voice above them said gruffly, 'Close on half an hour since it happened, sir.'

'Rig me some sort of screen, will you?' Josh was pulling the woman's clothes back out of the way. 'Get a set of emergency gear from the ambulance – she's going to deliver – we'll never get her to the hospital before she does – Nurse – here – '

He indicated to Bridget, with a curt gesture of his head, to come to the other side of him.

'Hold that leg – hold her, do you hear? Bend the knee – that's it – here, you – ' The young policeman who had been standing on the other side dropped to his knees on the other side of the woman, who was moaning again, her neck once more extended in a long arc. 'Hold that leg – like Nurse is – bend the knee –that's it – now hold her – other hand on her pelvis – at the side – hold her firm – got her?'

The policeman who had gone for the emergency case reappeared out of the fog, and with quick fingers, Josh undid the covers, and with careful movements, opened the packets inside.

'Bloody sterile this'll be,' he muttered. Then, as the woman once more stiffened and let her moans rise to a scream, said loudly, 'Easy does it, lovey, easy does it – we've got you – '

He fumbled in his pocket for his stethoscope, and with a swift movement, pushed the woman's torn clothes away, and set the bell on to the high dome of the abdomen.

'Foetal heart's all right – thank God for that – and here's another contraction – '

Bridget watched him, her heart pounding in her chest, as he pulled a pair of gloves from the emergency pack on to his wide hands, and heard him tell the woman, 'Now, listen, lovey, take it easy. I'm going to examine you – see how near this babe of yours is – easy now – ' and his hands moved gently but firmly, as he felt for the baby's head, while Bridget held on to one leg, and the young policeman, head averted, hung on grimly on the other side.

'Ye gods, she's crowning – ' Josh said loudly. 'Here we go – ' and under Bridget's terrified stare, the crumpled scalp, with black hair lying on it in even waves, like those left in beach sand when the tide goes out, appeared. The woman stretched herself again, pushed her legs hard against Bridget and the policeman, and the rest of the head appeared, the face looking furiously angry in its crumpled dusky redness.

There was an apparently interminable pause, and then, as the woman gave a deep grunt of intense effort, the rest of the baby's body appeared, the cord attached to its abdomen thick and gleaming in the glare of the spotlight. Josh held it high, both feet firm in a brown-gloved hand, and the baby squirmed, opened its wide, red mouth, and squalled lustily, its head held back in a sort of imitation of its mother's position just before it was born.

'It's a boy – a right lusty little so-and-so, too,' Josh

154

said exultantly, grinning from ear to ear in relief that the child was all right. 'Hear that, mother, lovey? It's a fine boy! Prem, but a good six-pounder, I'll bet – here, Bridget – give me a towel from the pack.'

And Bridget did, and held it carefully as Josh laid the still-squalling baby into it, to wrap him carefully, and hold him still, while Josh clipped and cut the cord.

'Give him to his mother,' he said. 'And tell her to hang on. We'd better deliver the placenta before we move her, if we can – '

And gently, Bridget knelt on the muddy grass of the verge, the fog moving sluggishly round her, to lay the baby beside his mother, who was now lying, her head at rest at last, with closed eyes in her white face.

'There he is, my dear,' Bridget whispered, and the woman opened her eyes, and looked at her, and then at the baby, wonderingly.

'All – all right?' she whispered, and as the baby opened his mouth to shout his rage at his unceremonious arrival, Bridget smiled and said, 'Listen to him – '

The woman's face lit into sudden brilliance, and she fumbled for the child, to peer eagerly into his creased face, to touch the streaked cheeks with a gentle finger.

'Here's the placenta – ' Josh said at length, as the woman gave one more effortful grunt, and then he worked in silence for a while, eventually to stand up and sign to the ambulance man on the other side of the hastily rigged tarpaulin screen.

'Get her back to the hospital fast, will you?' he said. 'Got an ambulance to spare?'

The man nodded. 'Three more just got here. This is the last case, anyway – we've got all the others away. You comin' back with us?'

'If there's nothing else to do here – have the rest gone back?'

'Gone with their patients – and the dead ones – shocking business – shocking.'

Josh nodded. 'But at least we've got one extra – very much alive – listen to the little devil,' and the baby squalled louder.

Together, Bridget and Josh rode back to the hospital, sitting beside the sleeping and exhausted mother, while Bridget cradled the baby warmly in her arms. And when Josh caught her eye, and smiled at her, his face warm, and with a question on it, she dropped her eyes, to look at the baby's crumpled little face. She could not look at Josh for the life of her.

Chapter 13

When they got back to the hospital, Casualty was seething with activity. Every cubicle was full, every one of the staff, including a few extra nurses collected from less busy parts of the hospital, running about as though all the hounds of hell were after them. In the waiting-room, two trolleys with grimly covered shapes on them, waited for porters to take them to the mortuary, and a theatre trolley arrived to take the most severely injured straight to Theatre, just as Bridget and Josh and their two patients arrived to swell the throng.

The RSO, his hair ruffled and his face creased with fatigue, took one look at the small bundle Bridget was carrying, and his face dropped.

'Christ, not a *baby* as well. Was it injured?'

Josh grinned. 'Looks fine to me. Born on the edge of the road – '

'That's all that I was short of,' the RSO said wearily. 'How's the mum?'

'Pretty exhausted – but as far as I could tell, no other injuries. Bloody miracle – '

'Mmm. Look, don't bring 'em in here. Get her straight to Maternity – tell them to put her in a single room and barrier nurse until they're sure she hasn't picked up an infection – '

'I should think she must have done. I mean, delivery in the gutter isn't exactly an aseptic technique,' Josh said.

'Yup – tell the Maternity people to put her on

penicillin. I'll send a radiographer up to take some films – better make sure she's got no bones broken – and I'll come and see her as soon as I can. Oh, and the baby'd better be in isolation, too.'

'It's prem – about thirty-two weeks maturity, to look at it.'

'Well, the midwives'll know whether it needs an incubator. Get them off, will you, Josh? I'm a bit pushed here – ' and he disappeared back into a cubicle, to deal with the motor-cyclist, who was now regaining consciousness, and making a great deal of noise about it.

Josh turned to where Bridget was standing, still clutching the baby, and said crisply, 'Right. You go on ahead, will you? I'll follow with Mum – '

The midwife on night duty looked startled, to say the least, when a trousered and dirty-faced Bridget arrived with a baby wrapped in a now oil-stained towel. Until she saw the look on the midwife's face, Bridget had no idea how very odd she looked, but she caught a reflection of herself in the glass front of a cupboard, and despite her fatigue, grinned slightly as she handed the baby over to the midwife.

'Mother's on the way – ' she began, and then the trolley with Josh at the head came rattling along the corridor from the lift. Succinctly, he gave his instructions to the midwife, who with a nod, swept into efficient action. Just as the trolley was being wheeled into one of the single wards at the side of the corridor, the mother turned her head, and putting her hand out, touched Bridget.

'Nurse?' she whispered hoarsely. 'Are you a nurse? The one who was with me?'

Bridget smiled, and held the hand warmly. 'Yes – and the doctor's here, too.'

The woman turned to look at Josh, and murmured, 'Thank you – thank you. Is – he all right?'

'I think he is, lovey,' Josh said, smiling down at her. 'He looked fine to me. They'll have a good look at him here, and tell you all about him properly – but I don't think you need worry – '

She bit her lip, to stop herself from crying tears of weakness and sheer happiness. 'What's your name, Doctor?'

He grinned widely. 'Joshua, I'm afraid.

'And yours, Nurse?'

'Bridget Preston.'

And the woman nodded. 'That's what I'll call him then. Joshua Preston Burke. Nice name. Thank you both so much – '

And the midwife pushed her away to her warm bed and to the rest she so sorely needed.

There was a long pause, then Josh said softly, 'There. A baby named after us. Isn't that nice? An – omen, perhaps?'

But Bridget turned away, and began to walk towards the lift. He fell into step beside her, and said softly, 'Bridget? Tiddler?' She shook her head wordlessly. All that had happened the night before, so very long ago now, it seemed, his letter and the way it had made her feel, the conversation with Bobby, came back to her, and misery washed over like a palpable thing.

But before she could open the lift gates, he took her arms, and pulled her away, leading her into the small linen room that was alongside.

He stood with his back to the door, and said firmly, 'Now, listen. I know it's the middle of the night – damn' near morning – and we're both dead on our feet'– his voice softened – 'you look exhausted, my love – ' and she turned away, and shook her head again.

' – but I *must* talk to you. I must. You – got my note?'

She swallowed, and then said huskily, 'Yes, I got it.'

'Well?' and his voice was urgent. 'Well?'

'Please, let me go. I – I'm tired,' she said.

'So am I,' he said grimly. 'And another few minutes

won't make much odds. Please, Tiddler, what have you to say about that note?'

And his voice, the nearness of him, was too much for her exhausted body to cope with any more. She felt huge tearing sobs start deep in her throat, felt her shoulders shake, and leaning against the little table covered with sheets and towels in the middle of the room, wept as though her tears would tear her apart.

His arms were round her then, holding her close, holding her against the roughness of his tweed jacket, holding her shoulders so that their shaking was stilled, so that she felt warm and safe again.

Slowly, the tears subsided, and she managed to pull away from him, to stand pressed against the wall as far away from him as she could get.

'You lied to me. You lied to me,' she said flatly, and her eyes were huge in her pinched face.

'I lied to you?' He looked genuinely puzzled. 'Lied? My love, what about? I told you all I could tell you in that letter – that was why I wrote it – to – clear the slate – to start new – '

But she shook her head stubbornly. 'You lied,' she said again, feeling the dreary persistence in her voice. 'I know now.'

'Know what?'

And at the continued puzzlement in his voice she became angry, and clenched her fists and almost shook them at him.

'I saw her last night – Bobby – and she *told* me – '

His own eyes glittered at that. 'Bobby? She told you something last night?'

'Yes!' she blazed. 'So you can keep your lies for *her* in future. I want no part of it – '

His hand shot out, and gripped her wrist in a grasp so strong it hurt her, and he bent his head close to hers, and looked directly into her eyes, eyes full of pain, and anger.

160

'I don't know what she told you – that girl is a pathological liar – but whatever it is, *I* told you the truth in my letter. You *must* believe that – '

She closed her eyes wearily. 'Oh, God, I don't know what to believe – I just don't know – '

He dropped her hand, and stood back, then after a moment said shortly, 'We're both tired out. And the only way I'll ever convince you is to get this business about Bobby sorted out properly once and for all. Tomorrow – today – we'll go and see her – '

'No – no, I couldn't – not again – '

'Yes!' He almost shouted it at her. 'Yes! Together, we'll go and see her. And then you'll find out for certain. Now, go to bed. And at two o'clock this afternoon, I'm coming to the Home to collect you and we'll go over to Sick Bay and see that – girl. And if you aren't waiting for me, so help me God, I'll come and drag you out of your room – and don't think I don't mean it.'

And he turned on his heel and left her, listening to the lift clatter away to the third floor and the doctors' quarters.

It was half past one in the afternoon when she woke from a thick and troubled sleep to find one of the Home maids standing grinning down at her.

' 'Allo, Nurse – 'ow are yer, love? Better for a good kip, I'll be bound – ' she plonked a tray of tea and toast down on the bedside-table and crossed the room to open the curtains. As the afternoon sun came streaming in, Bridget blinked, and rubbed her face, aware of the stiffness of fatigue that was still in her.

'Cor, but you're a right one, you and your pal, aren't yer? Evenin' papers is full of it – two plucky little nurses from the Royal, that's what it says, two plucky little nurses, and three doctors all out in the fog in the middle of the night, savin' lives – an' that baby – ain't that a thing though? Was 'e a nice baby?'

'Very nice,' Bridget said absently. 'The papers?'

The maid grinned, basking in the reflected glory of it all.

'Not 'arf! All over the front pages it is – not much other news about, see? Makes quite a story. They had men 'ere today – wanting pictures of you and Nurse Jessolo, but Matron wasn't havin' any. "They're sleepin'," she told 'em, "and they're not to be disturbed," that's what she said. And 'ome Sister says to tell yer you're off duty rest of today, and not to go back till termorrer mornin'. So you just drink your tea and have a bite o' that there toast, and rest up. Lovely day, too – bit of an airin'd do you all the good in the world,' and she bustled away to tell the other maids about the way poor little Nurse Preston looked when she woke for her tea and toast.

Bridget swallowed her tea and toast with a relish that almost surprised her, and then took a hot bath that brought some of the exhaustion out with the steam. She dressed slowly, and was still combing her hair when the maid reappeared, grinning even more widely, if that were possible.

'There's someone waitin' downstairs for you. An' 'e says to tell yer if yer don't come down right now, 'e'll be up 'ere to get you. 'E's standin' on the bottom step, and 'e looks as if 'e means it – ain't 'e a looker, though? Smashin' feller – you'd better 'urry, Nurse. If 'e comes up 'ere 'ome Sister'll 'ave you on toast – '

And under the grinning maid's eye, Bridget couldn't help herself.

She walked down the stairs with all the dignity she could muster, all too aware of the maid watching her from the landing at the top.

He was standing as the maid had said, staring up at her as she came, his hair neat, his face fresh-shaven, looking as rested as though he had spent the past twenty-four hours in bed, rather than a bare five or six.

'Hello,' he said softly. 'How are you?'

'Very well, thank you,' she said stiffly.

He took her arm, and then walked out of the Home into the garden, and by one of the benches, he stopped and pulled her down to sit beside him.

'Will you come to see Bobby, Tiddler?'

She looked up at him, startled.

'You're – asking me? I thought – '

'I'm not going to force you to do anything against your will,' he said soberly. 'Last night – this morning – I was tired, and – upset – you seemed so – so bitter about me. But now – well, if you don't want to come, I won't force you. But I do ask this. I've told you one thing. Clearly, Bobby's told you another. And though it hurts to have to admit it, there's no reason why you should believe me rather than her. I've not exactly shown myself to be – a suitor *sans reproche*. On past showing, you're entitled to believe me a liar as well as – a tom-cat – '

She winced at that. 'Don't – '

He laughed a bitter little laugh. 'Well, wasn't I? It was your own term – you used it to Bobby, and my God, you were right to – no, I shouldn't say that. Whatever else Bobby may be, I've no right to call her names. I – was as much a party to her behaviour as she was herself, I suppose – '

He looked at her, and smiled crookedly. 'I don't like myself too well, at present, Tiddler. It never mattered before, you see. But now, I feel – ' and he moved his shoulders in a gesture of distaste.

She sat in silence, looking with unseeing eyes at the wide lawn, the early flowers nodding in their beds, at the thin spring sunshine glancing off the white-painted walls of the garden. Then she said, with sudden resolve, 'You're quite right. Of course you are. The only thing to do is go and see Bobby – and – ' She stopped, and looked at him, smiling a little. 'I – want to know. It's – important to me. I'm feeling less emotional this morning – afternoon, I mean – than I was. Last night I hated you – '

'And now?' He put his hand out, and held her chin between strong warm fingers. 'And now?'

She bit her lip, not meeting his gaze. 'Now, I – I want to know.'

'Come on, then. We'll get it over – '

They walked in silence across the courtyard, managing to avoid the few nurses and doctors who seemed to want to stop and talk to them about the night's exploits, and still in silence, walked along the corridor that led to the sick bay.

Bridget felt herself go cold again, a familiar sick feeling, as she thought of having to see Bobby again. And Josh would be with Bobby again, just as he used to be. She stole a look at him, at the rigid face, as he walked head high, beside her, and told herself – no. He'll be there, but not as it used to be.

Sister on sick bay looked at them curiously when they arrived and asked to see Nurse Aston. But she gave her permission, and watched them covertly as they went down the little corridor to the room at the end. She would have given a great deal to have been able to hear what was going on there – and wished, not for the first time, that the sick bay was an ordinary ward, instead of single rooms. It would have given her a better opportunity to 'keep an eye on things' as she told herself mendaciously.

It was Josh who knocked at the door, who opened it in response to the high 'Come in!' in Bobby's unmistakable voice. And it was Josh who walked in first, while Bridget, her nervousness rising in a huge wave, lingered behind for a second.

She heard the warmth, the almost caressing note in Bobby's voice as she said in surprised delight, 'Josh!' and wanted to turn and run.

But Josh stood aside, and put a strong hand out, and led her in so that she was standing beside him in the door-way, looking across at Bobby in her nest of pillows.

164

She was looking better than she had – or perhaps that was because Bridget had already seen the change in her, and could no longer be shocked by it. Her hair was tied back with a wide, blue ribbon, which gave her an appealing little-girl look, and the matching bed jacket showed off her fair skin to advantage.

But when she saw Bridget, her face altered, the warm welcoming smile that had wreathed her lips giving way to a sort of petulant surprise.

'Bridget?' she said uncertainly. 'You here again – '

Josh closed the door firmly, and said evenly, 'Yes, Bobby. Again. And I want you to repeat to her again whatever it was you told her last night. Now. While I'm here to listen.'

Bobby stared at him, and frowned sharply. 'For heaven's sake, Josh, what is all this? If I say anything to Bridget, it's my affair – I don't see that it's anything to do with you – '

'I rather think it is,' he said, and stood still, his hands in his white-coat pockets, his head bent in a watchful way. 'I rather think it is. Will you repeat whatever it was?'

She slid down in her bed a little, and made a *moué*. 'Why should I? Anyway, it was true – ' but she sounded unconvinced.

He looked at her with distaste, his mouth turned down. Then without turning his gaze away from Bobby, he said softly, 'Bridget, will *you* tell me now what Bobby told you last night?'

She gasped a little, looked at him appealingly, and for a fleeting moment, he looked at her, his eyes stern.

There was a long silence, then, almost against her will, Bridget heard her own voice.

'Bobby says the – the baby she got rid of was yours. That you knew. That you knew she was going to get rid of it, and that she did it for your sake.'

The silence this time was electric, and Bridget felt, rather than saw, the muscles of Josh's face go hard as

165

he clenched his teeth. Then, in a voice thin with the control he was putting into it, he said slowly, 'That baby could not have been mine. On your own admission, Bobby, you were three months pregnant. The – the last time I – could have been responsible was well before three months ago. According to your history, and the information you eventually gave the Gynae registrar, that child was conceived at about Christmas-time.'

Bobby said nothing, lying quite still, staring at him with her shadowed eyes, her mouth a thin line.

'And you know as well as I do what happened at Christmas. When Bridget left the house that night, I went shortly afterwards – and very angry indeed you were about it. What happened that night, Bobby? Because it was then, wasn't it?'

Still she said nothing, only lying still and staring at him unwinkingly.

'I know what happened that night, Bobby. You don't need to tell me. Because you forget that David Nestor was not a man to care what he told to who. You know that, don't you? One of the boasters, David?'

Bobby closed her eyes at that, 'No – '

'Yes – yes; Bobby, he told me. With a great deal of relish. As he put it, I'd – "spoiled his weekend" ' – his voice grated in anger – 'so he sorted out things for himself. Didn't he –? And until you were brought in that night last week and I was sent to see you, I had not the least idea of what had happened – not that you were pregnant, or what you had done about it – '

Bobby pulled herself up then, to lean forwards, her face twisted with rage.

'All right – all right – ' she screamed. 'So what? So bloody what? You walked out and left me high and dry, to run after your sweet little – bitch'– she almost spat the word – 'so what would you expect? And who cares, anyway? What's it to do with you? Don't tell me I was the first – or that I'm the last either – ' and she looked at Bridget with such loathing and such spite in her eyes, that Bridget shrank back in sick fear.

Josh was breathing hard now, and put a hand out to hold on to Bridget, filling her with strength as he touched her.

'I'm sorry, Bobby,' he said. 'Very sorry. Not just because – of what's happened to you, but because of the sort of person you are. You'll never be happy, will you? Not unless the world always goes your way. And I doubt if it will. It hasn't this time – I had an affair with you, and it ended – a long time ago. And it's no good trying to pick up the pieces, because there aren't any left. I – ' He looked down at Bridget. 'We both wish you well, Bobby, believe it or not. Don't we?' and he looked at Bridget again. But she couldn't move or speak, just standing still and silent beside him.

'I'm sorry,' he said again. 'Sorry to have made you – admit all this to both of us. But I had to. Goodbye, Bobby – ' and with a gentle pressure on Bridget's arm, he opened the door, and led her out, closing it behind him with a sharp click.

Bridget stood in silence beside him for a long moment, ignoring the curious stare of the nurse who rustled past on her way to the sluice at the end. Then she looked up at Josh and said miserably, 'That – that was horrible.'

'We can't talk here,' he said, and moving purposefully led the way back down the corridor towards the main courtyard and the Home garden.

Neither of them said a word as they walked, and the silence persisted even after they were back on the little wooden bench under the tree, back among the spring flowers and the sound of birds twittering desultorily above the distant roar of traffic from the main road far beyond them.

Then Bridget said again, as though there had been no gap at all, 'Horrible – '

'I suppose you're thinking I'm a – pretty dreadful

person. To have made Bobby tell you that way?' he said, his voice expressionless.

She remembered the look of anger on Bobby's face, the shrill sound of her voice, and said heavily, 'She's – had enough to cope with. No matter what else she may have done, she's had a lot to cope with. And now – it was like – oh, I don't know. Like standing by and jeering while somebody was whipped – '

'I know, I know,' he said roughly. 'But it was the only way. She's a devious person, Bridget. Bobby can't tell the truth, even if she tries. She tailors what she says to each occasion and the person she is talking to. And the only way to convince you of what happened was to put her in a situation where she couldn't lie. Which was why I did it.'

Bridget moved fretfully.

'I don't understand – I don't understand,' she said. 'The night she had her operation – you were so – miserable – so distressed. I thought – I thought it was because you loved her. That you – cared. And now this – '

'Of course I was distressed – of course I cared. Damn it, I'm a doctor! Do you think I *liked* what I saw when I examined her that night? Liked to do a hysterectomy on a girl of her age? I'd have to be – a completely callous person not to have cared – and though I may sound a bit callous about her now, I still care about what's happened to her,' he said savagely.

She closed her eyes against the brightness of the sunshine, and said miserably, 'What *will* happen to Bobby, Josh? What will happen to her now?'

'Oh, God, I don't know!' He sounded irritable suddenly. 'Who can say? She's – promiscuous, immoral – who can say what will happen to her?'

'And you don't care.' It wasn't a question. Just a statement.

'I – can't pretend I do, not now, apart from – the

168

medical aspect,' he said with painful honesty. 'For me, as a person, rather than as a doctor, she was – an episode. Just an episode. I'm sorry for her, in a remote sort of way – but that's all.'

She leaned back on the hardness of the wooden bench, and looked down at her hands twisted on her lap.

'And what will I be? Another – episode?'

He twisted in his seat then, to sit close beside her, to hold her chin in his hand again, forcing her to look at him.

'No, my love. You – you're special. Even if you decide right now not to have any more to do with me, if you get up and walk away from me at this moment, you'll always be special to me. Do you believe that? Can you believe that?'

She sat very still, feeling the warmth and strength of his fingers on her face, seeing the truth of what he said in his eyes, in the set of his wide mouth, tracing every line of his face with her own eyes. Then she said tremulously, 'I've got to believe you – I've got to – '

'Got to?' and his voice was infinitely gentle.

'I love you, Josh,' she said simply, and looked at him with a clear look that made him drop his own eyes, made him sit back on the wooden bench almost trembling, his hands lax on his white coated knees.

'Thank you – thank you,' he said at length, and then looked at her, his mouth twisted into a rueful half smile.

'That's a feeble thing to say – ' and he moved closer to her, to put his arm round her, so that they sat side by side in dumb happiness, the soft breeze moving her hair across his face, just sitting in a sort of exhausted peace.

He stirred at length, taking a deep breath.

'It's going to be wonderful, Tiddler. Wonderful,' and his voice had an exultant lilt in it. 'We'll be married – soon – we'll be married – '

'I – give me time, Josh – time – ' She felt a sudden wave of anxiety then. Married? It was what she wanted more

169

than anything in the world, but somehow, it couldn't be thought of. Not yet. Not too soon.

'I know,' he said softly. 'I know. You need time – to be sure – isn't that it?'

She nodded dumbly.

'Sure that I love you?' He sounded oddly mischievous, almost little-boy, and she laughed shakily in spite of herself.

'I think that *is* what I mean – ' She turned and looked up at him. 'I – I think I've loved you for a long time. A very long time – but – '

He smiled at her, all his love in his eyes, spilling over her in a wave of feeling that was almost a concrete thing. 'And I have loved you for a long time. And there's plenty more time. You'll see, my love, Bridget my love. You'll see – ' and at the confidence in his voice, she relaxed, to sit still in the circle of his arm, confident too, knowing that the future was opening before her, wide and full of the promise of all she had ever wanted.

And beyond the quiet garden, the hospital went on its own organised, impersonal way, offering life and death, beginnings and endings, to the people who came to it, the people who worked in it trying in the only way they knew how to comfort the sick, to give the peace and freedom from pain the sick demanded of them.

'Comfort,' Bridget said suddenly. 'I came here looking for comfort – I didn't know, but that was what I wanted – '

'You brought it with you,' he said softly. 'It's a two-way thing. You brought it with you – for me, for the people you looked after, for the people you worked with – '

'I shall go on nursing,' she said, with a sort of discovering in her voice. 'I want to go on – I will, won't I?'

'For a while,' he said. 'For a while. And then – ' He took a deep contented breath. 'No matter. There's all the time in the world to talk about it. All the time in the world – '

170